WIL/CH

We hope you enjoy this book.
Please return or renew it by the due date.
You can renew it at **www.norfolk.gov.uk/libraries**
or by using our free library app. Otherwise you can
phone **0344 800 8020** - please have your library
card and pin ready.
You can sign up for email reminders too.

UP NEXT >>>

:02   SPORTS ZONE SPECIAL REPORT

:04   **FEATURE PRESENTATION:**

POINT-BLANK PAINTBALL

FOLLOWED BY:

:50   SPORTS ZONE POSTGAME RECAP

:51   SPORTS ZONE POSTGAME EXTRA

:52   SI KIDS INFO CENTRE

SPORTS ZONE
SPECIAL REPORT

PNT
PAINTBALL
FBL
FOOTBALL
SKT
SKATEBOARDING
BSL
BASEBALL
BBL
BASKETBALL
HKY

TALENTED TWINS TO COMPETE FOR SOLE PLACE ON TOP TEAM!

PETER ECCLESTON

STATS:
ROLE: POINTMAN
AGE: 14
COLOURS: BLUE AND SILVER

BIO: Peter Eccleston is super-smart and ultra-organized on – and off – the paintball course. He prefers to play it cool and plan ahead, setting traps and preparing ambushes to catch his opponents off-guard.

NOAH ECCLESTON

STATS:
ROLE: MARKSMAN
AGE: 14
COLOURS: ORANGE AND GREEN

BIO: Noah Eccleston is as playful and rebellious as they come. Only his twin brother, Peter, can get this class clown to stop joking around and stay serious. While Peter prefers to hang back and pick off opponents one by one, trigger-happy Noah would rather charge forward and open fire on the competition.

Sports Illustrated KIDS

UP NEXT: POINT-BLANK PAINTBALL

JOSEPH ECCLESTON

BIO: Joseph Eccleston is the father of Peter and Noah. A successful businessman, Mr Eccleston believes that you can only count on yourself. He puts a lot of pressure on his sons to succeed, and insists they compete with each other at everything.

BLZ vs BNS
3-1
TGR vs ROR
33-32
EAG vs BAN
14-7
SPA vs WLD
4-3
BAN vs ROR
21-15
RZR vs LIG
4-3
BLZ vs BNS
3-1

JOHN PATTERSON

TEAM: ROYALS **AGE:** 37 **ROLE:** COACH

BIO: Coach Patterson is a three-time state paintball champion. He has a reputation for turning paintball rookies into pros.

COACH

SAM "KING" LIONEL

TEAM: ROYALS **AGE:** 15 **ROLE:** CO-CAPTAIN

BIO: A gifted sharpshooter, King rarely misses the mark. The Royals count on him to remain calm even under heavy enemy fire.

KING

CORA "QUEEN" RAMIREZ

TEAM: ROYALS **AGE:** 14 **ROLE:** CO-CAPTAIN

BIO: Cora "Queen" Ramirez is the brains behind the Royals. She's a gifted strategist and a natural born leader.

QUEEN

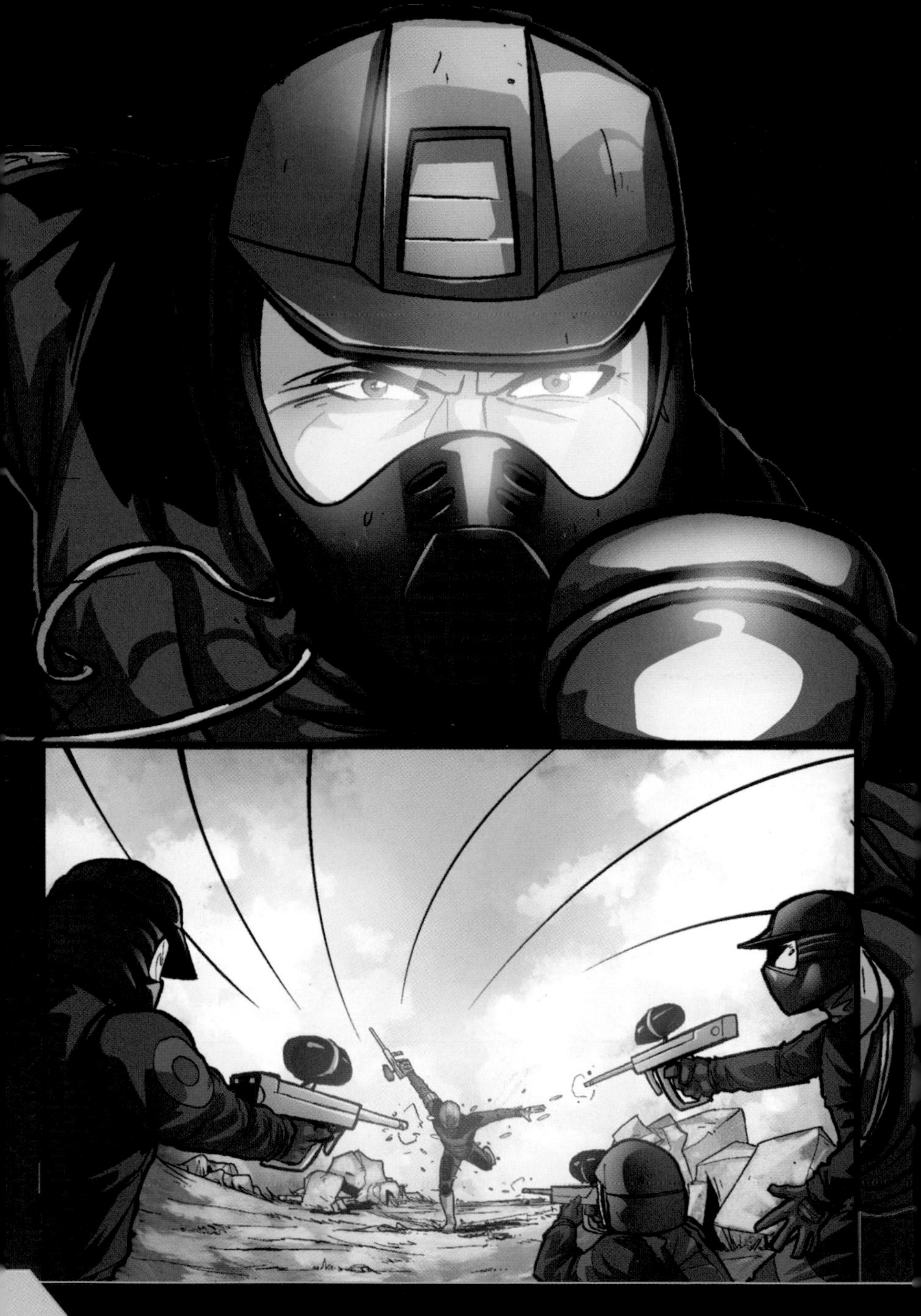

Sports Illustrated KIDS

PRESENTS

POINT-BLANK PAINTBALL

A PRODUCTION OF

raintree

a Capstone company — publishers for children

written by Scott Ciencin
illustrated by Aburtov
coloured by Fares Maese
Andres Esparza

designed and directed by Bob Lentz
edited by Sean Tulien
creative direction by Heather Kindseth
editorial direction by Michael Dahl

Raintree is an imprint of Capstone Global Library, a company incorporated in England and Wales having its registered office at 264 Banbury Road, Oxford, OX2 7DY – Registered company number: 6695582

www.raintree.co.uk
myorders@raintree.co.uk

ISBN: 978 1 4747 7159 7
22 21 20 19 18
10 9 8 7 6 5 4 3 2

British Library Cataloguing in Publication Data
A full catalogue record for this book is available from the British Library.

Originated by Capstone Global Library Ltd
Printed and bound in India

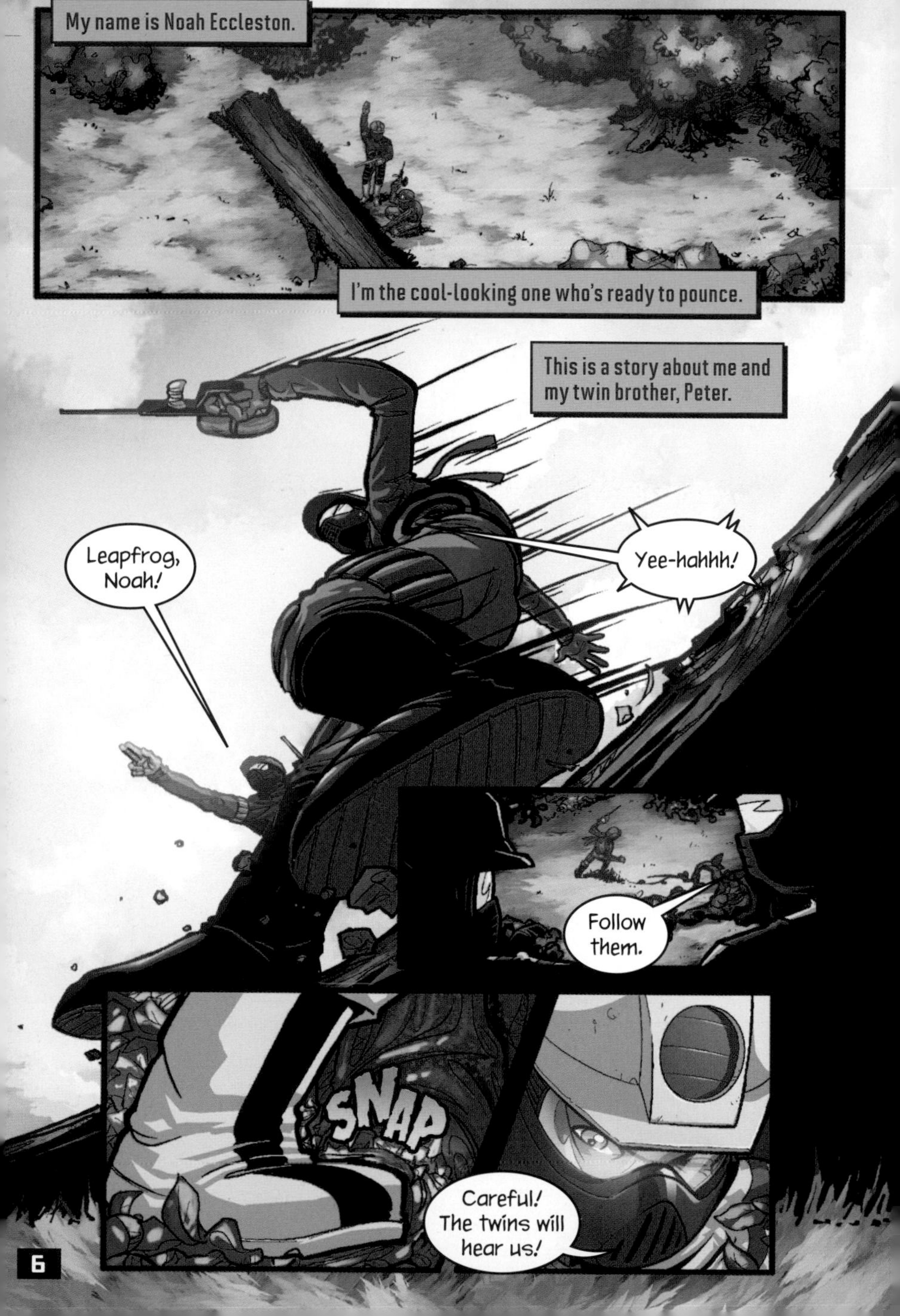
My name is Noah Eccleston.
I'm the cool-looking one who's ready to pounce.
This is a story about me and my twin brother, Peter.
Leapfrog, Noah!
Yee-hahhh!
Follow them.
SNAP
Careful! The twins will hear us!

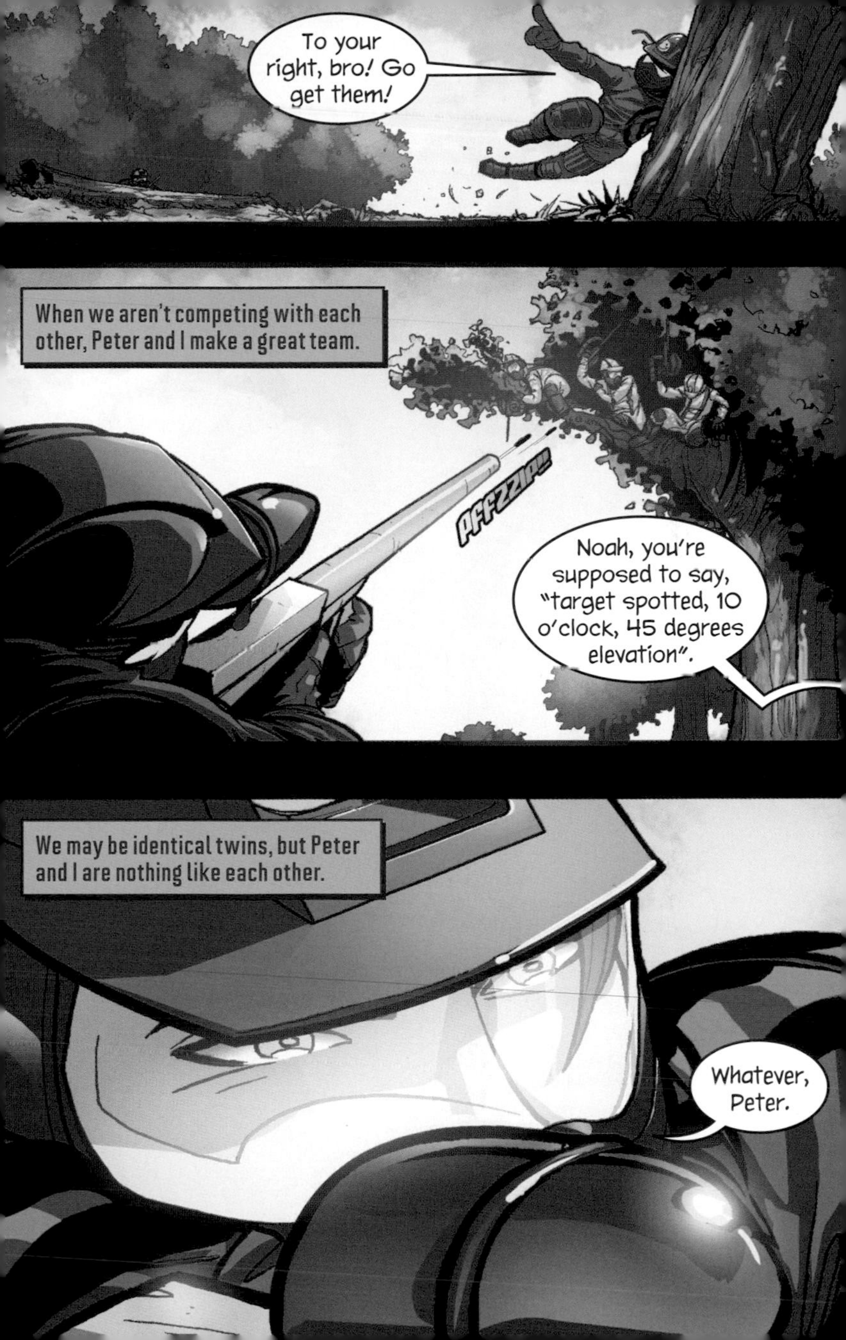
To your right, bro! Go get them!
When we aren't competing with each other, Peter and I make a great team.
PFFZZIP!!
Noah, you're supposed to say, "target spotted, 10 o'clock, 45 degrees elevation".
We may be identical twins, but Peter and I are nothing like each other.
Whatever, Peter.

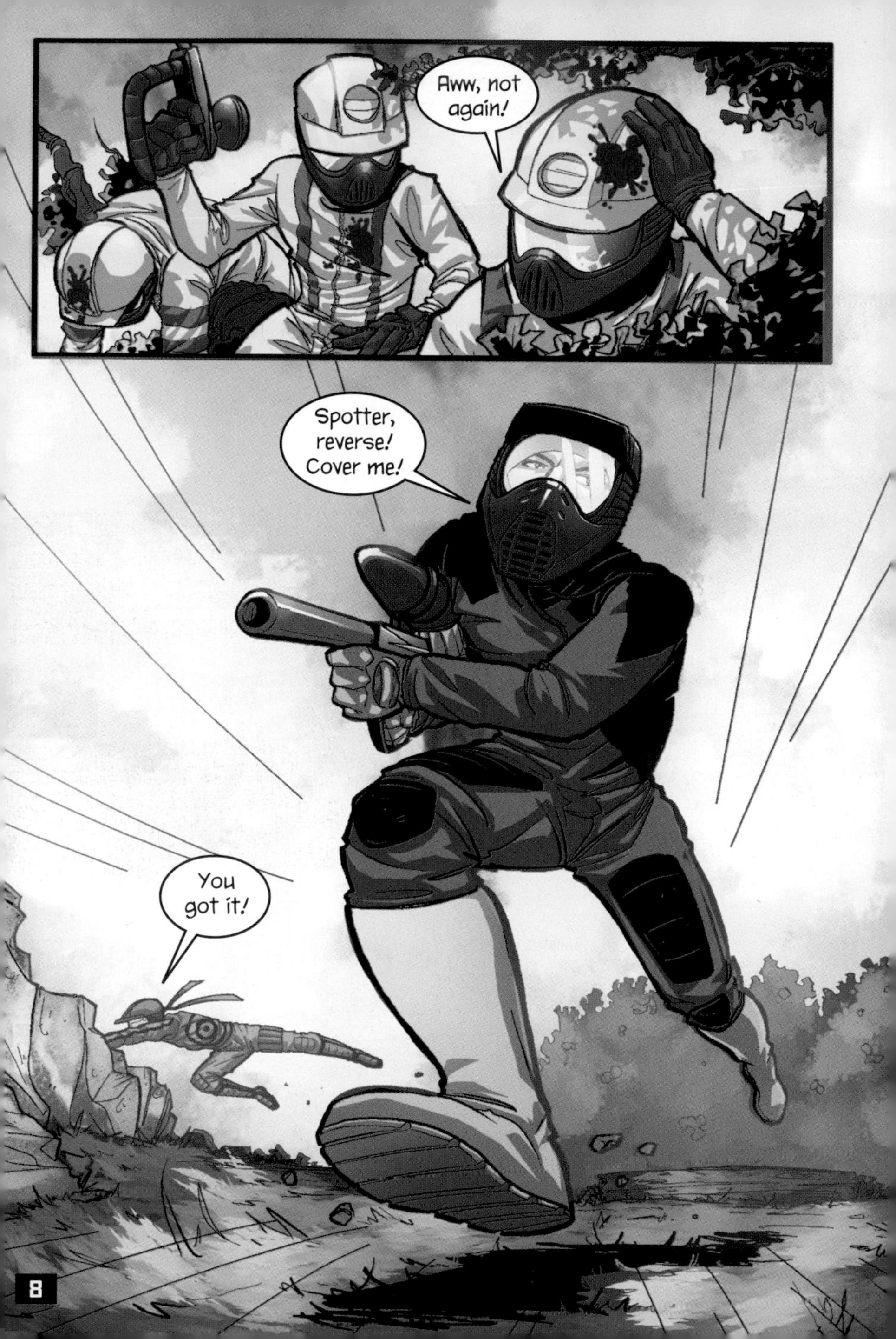
Aww, not again!
Spotter, reverse! Cover me!
You got it!

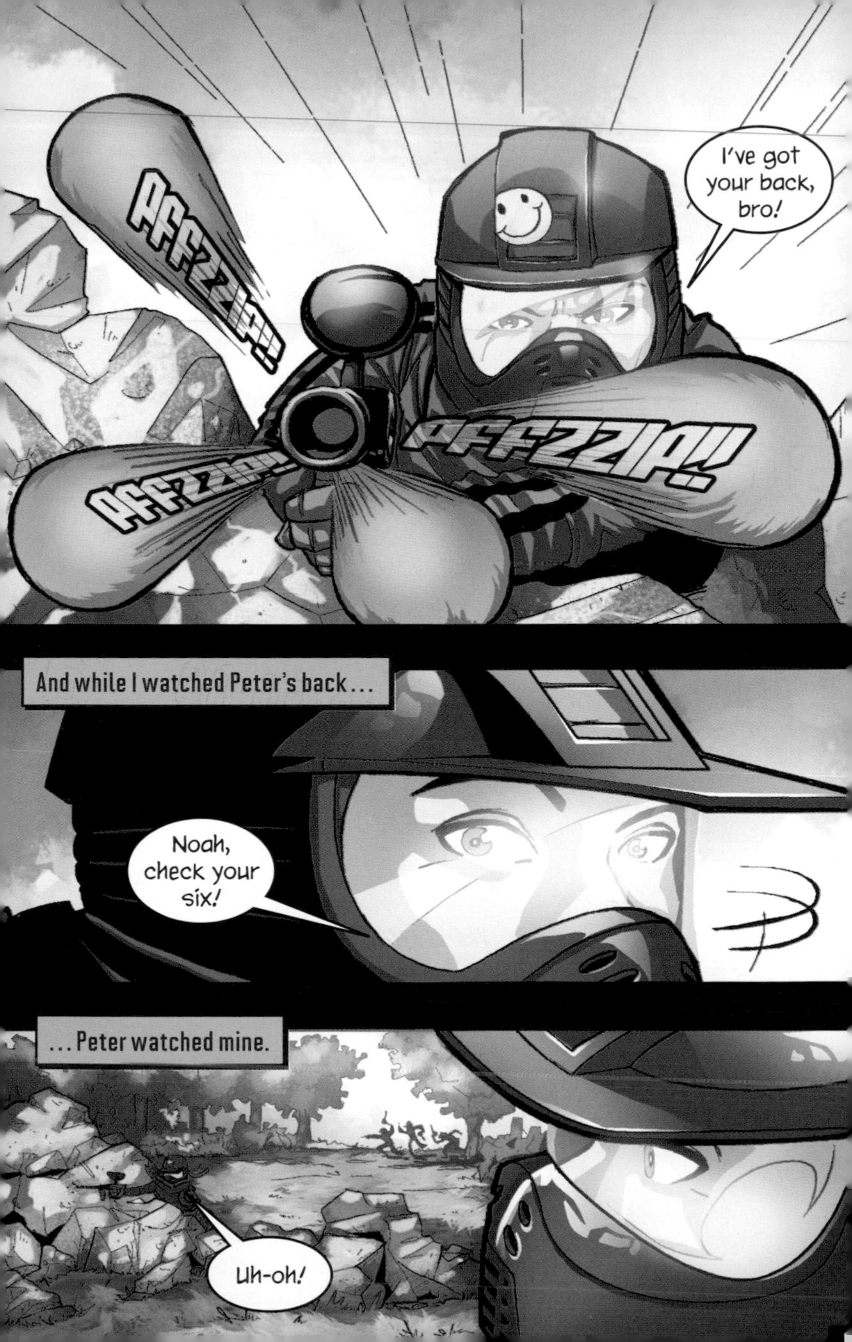
PFFZZIP!!
I've got your back, bro!
PFFZZIP!!
PFFZZIP!!
And while I watched Peter's back . . .
Noah, check your six!
. . . Peter watched mine.
Uh-oh!

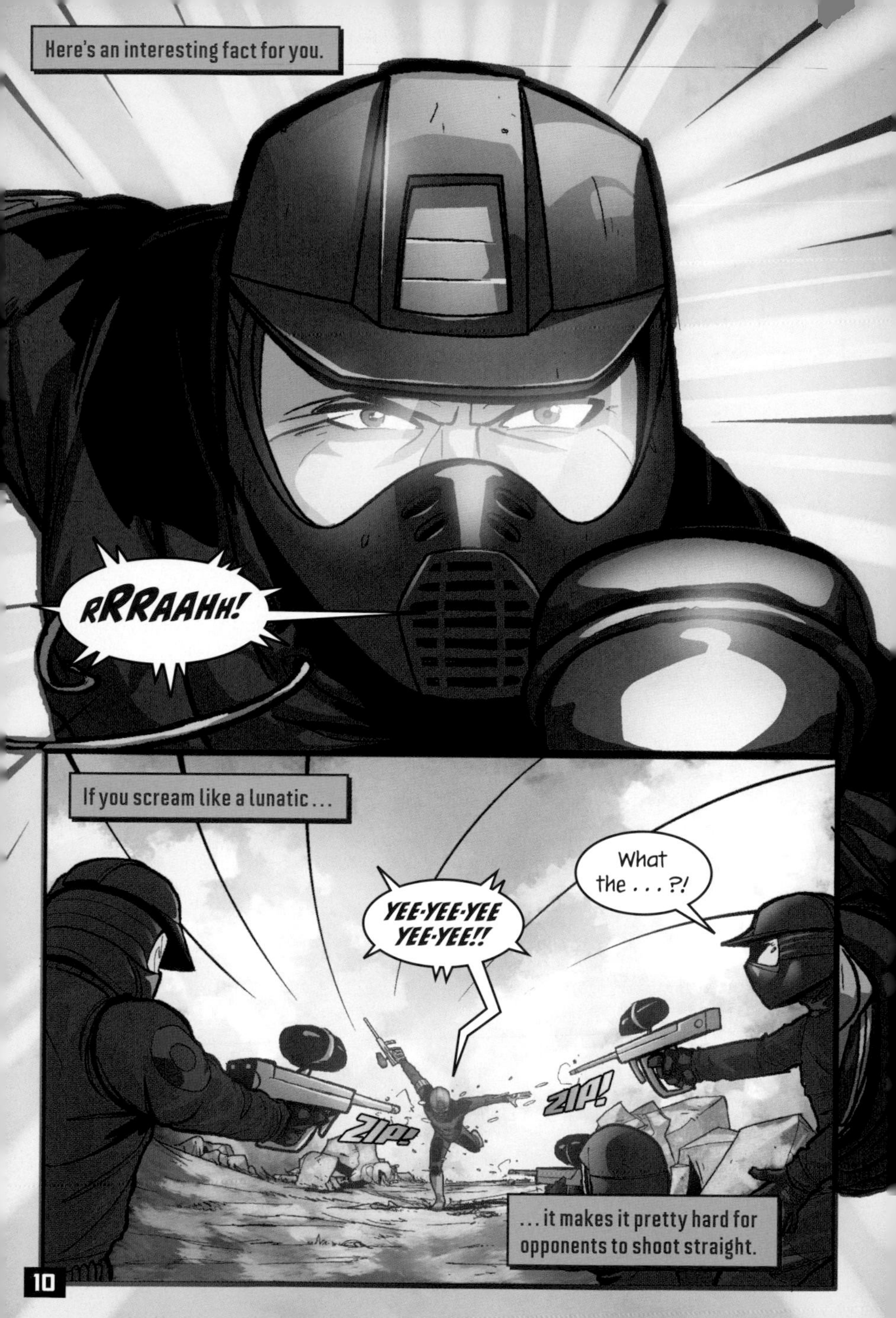
Here's an interesting fact for you.
RRRAAHH!
If you scream like a lunatic . . .
YEE-YEE-YEE YEE-YEE!!
What the . . . ?!
ZIP!
ZIP!
. . . it makes it pretty hard for opponents to shoot straight.

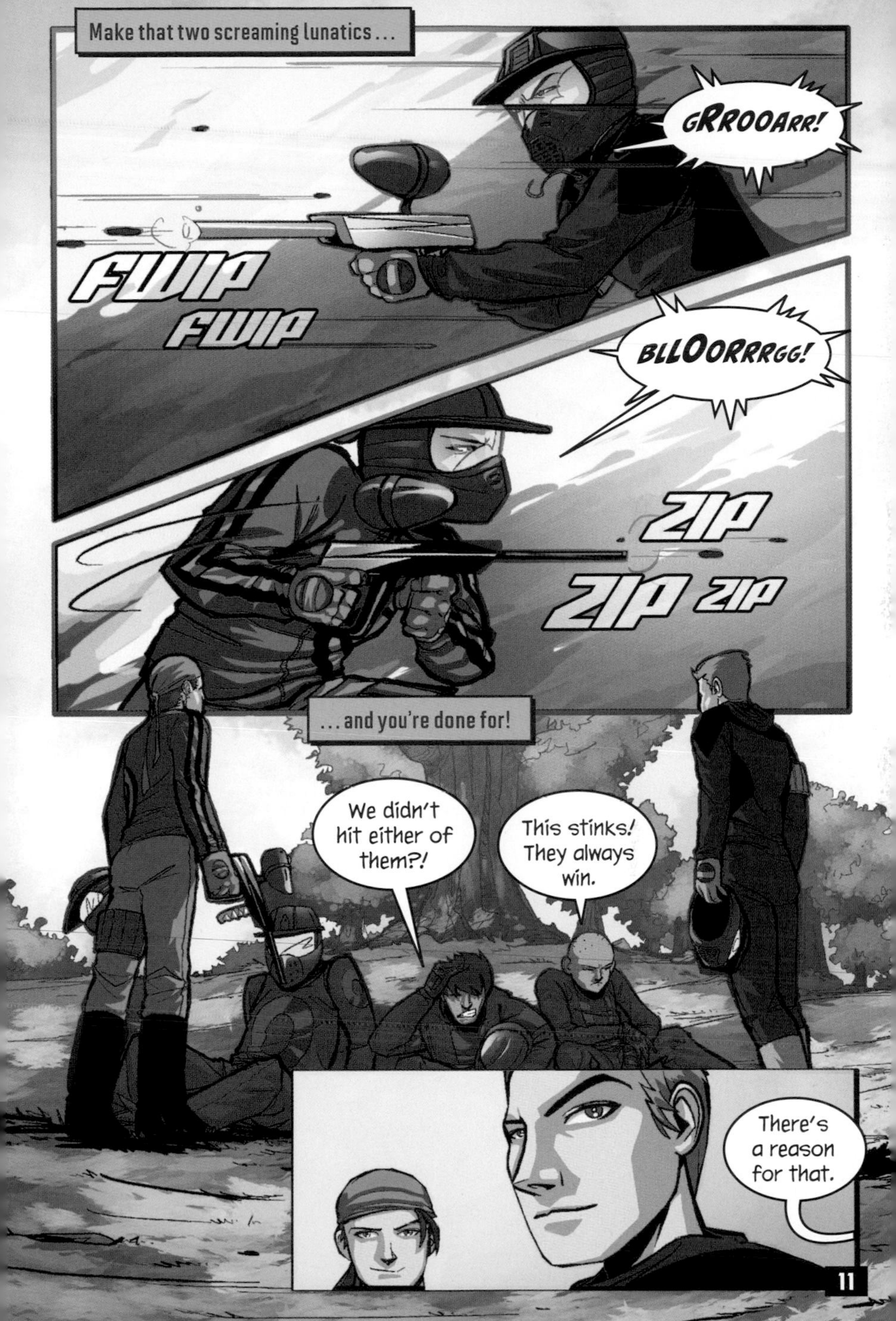
Make that two screaming lunatics . . .
GRROOARR!
FWIP
FWIP
BLLOORRRGG!
ZIP
ZIP ZIP
. . . and you're done for!
We didn't hit either of them?!
This stinks! They always win.
There's a reason for that.

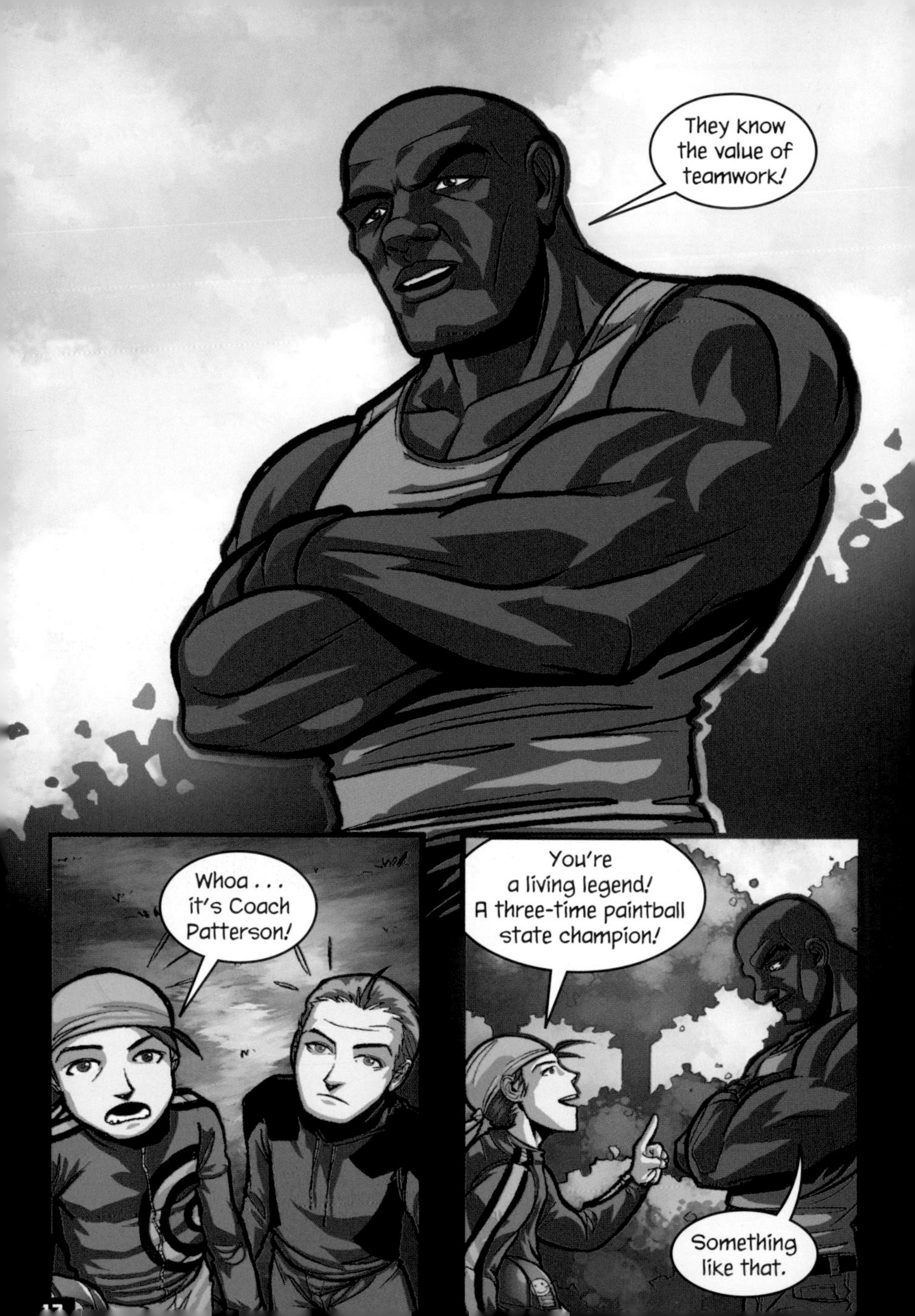
They know the value of teamwork!
Whoa . . . it's Coach Patterson!
You're a living legend! A three-time paintball state champion!
Something like that.

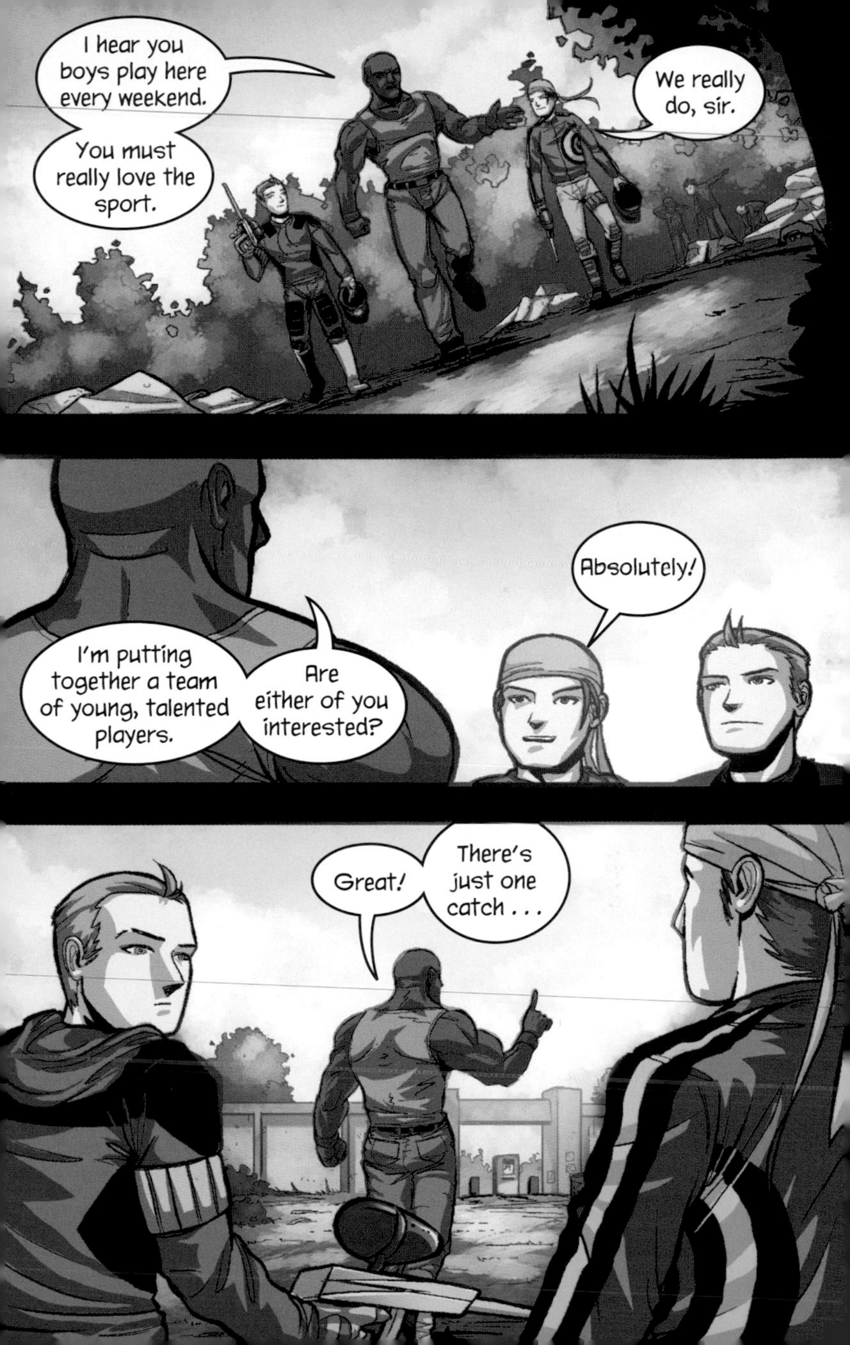
I hear you boys play here every weekend.
You must really love the sport.
We really do, sir.
I'm putting together a team of young, talented players.
Are either of you interested?
Absolutely!
Great!
There's just one catch . . .

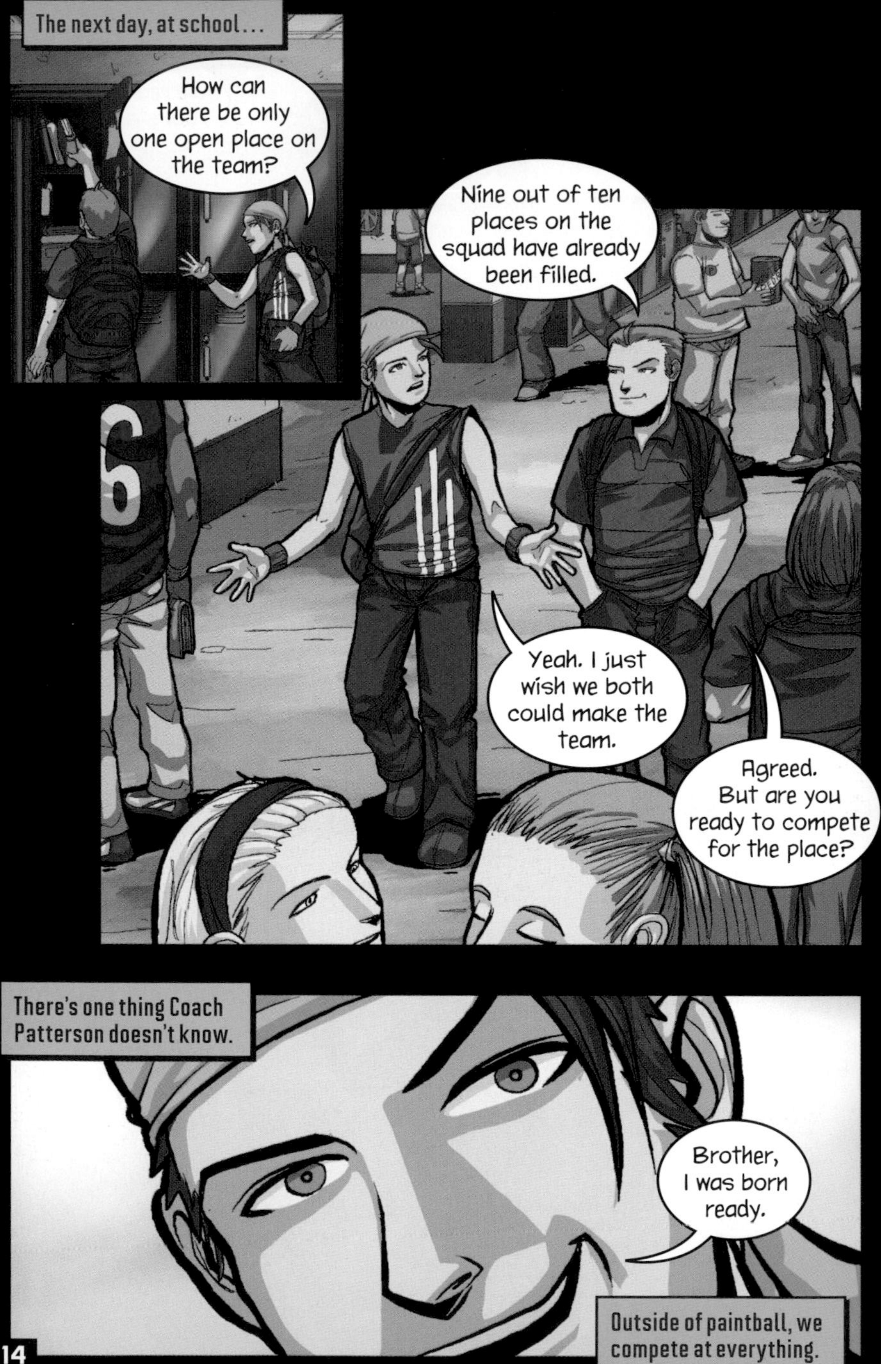
The next day, at school...
How can there be only one open place on the team?
Nine out of ten places on the squad have already been filled.
Yeah. I just wish we both could make the team.
Agreed. But are you ready to compete for the place?
There's one thing Coach Patterson doesn't know.
Brother, I was born ready.
Outside of paintball, we compete at everything.

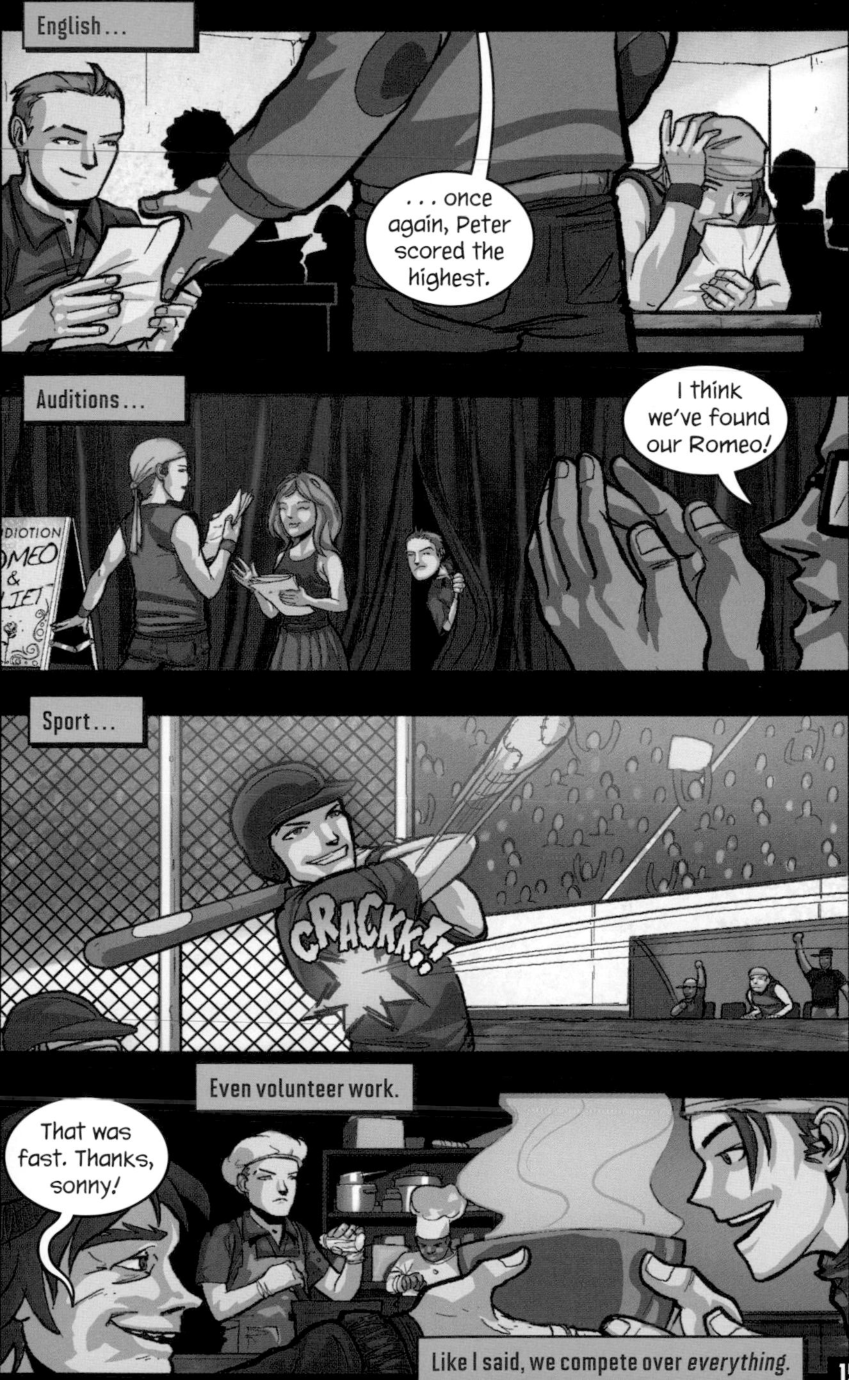

English...
. . . once again, Peter scored the highest.
Auditions...
I think we've found our Romeo!
Sport...
CRACKK!!
Even volunteer work.
That was fast. Thanks, sonny!
Like I said, we compete over *everything*.

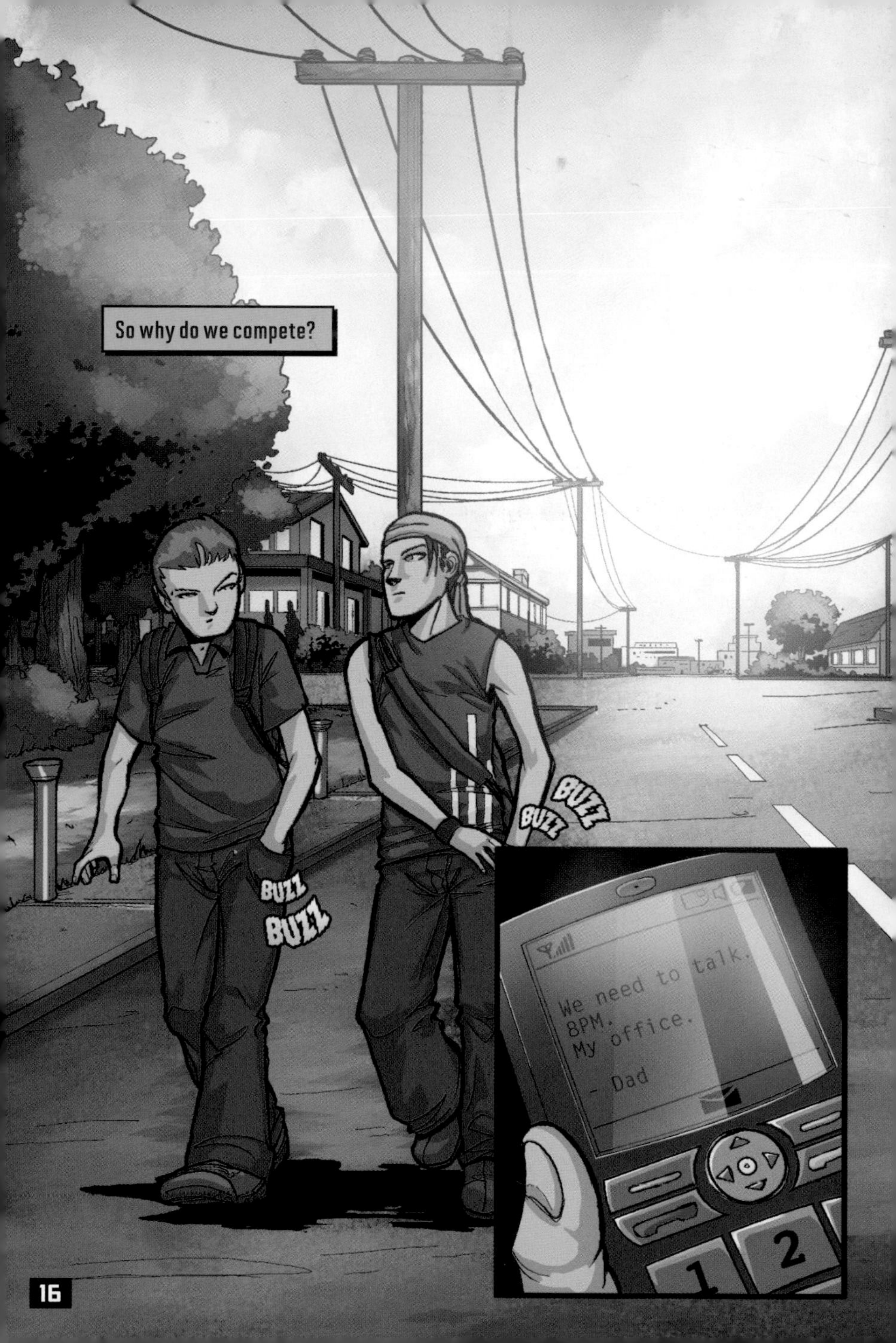
So why do we compete?
BUZZ
BUZZ
BUZZ
BUZZ
We need to talk.
8PM.
My office.
- Dad
1
2

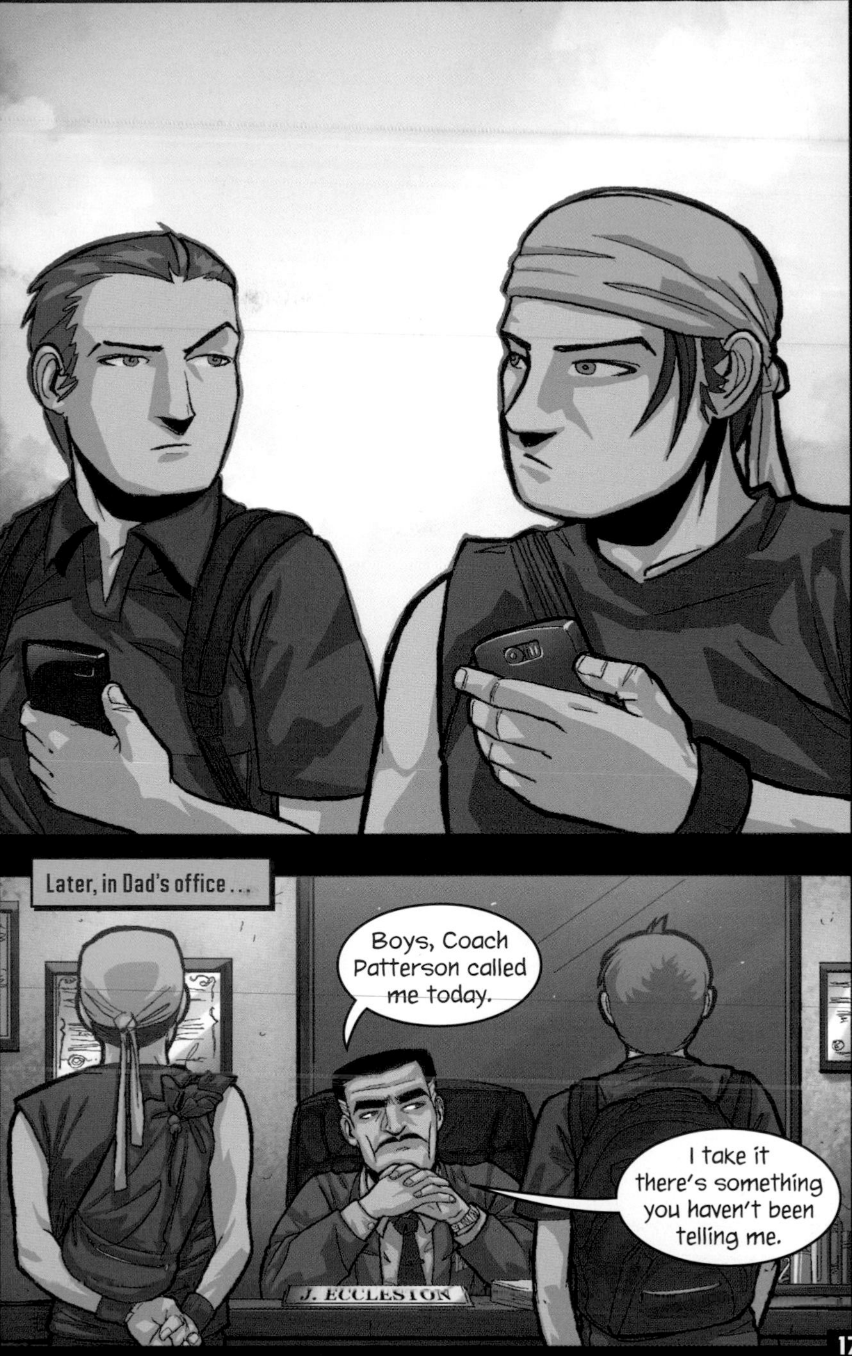
Later, in Dad's office . . .
Boys, Coach Patterson called me today.
I take it there's something you haven't been telling me.
J. ECCLESTON

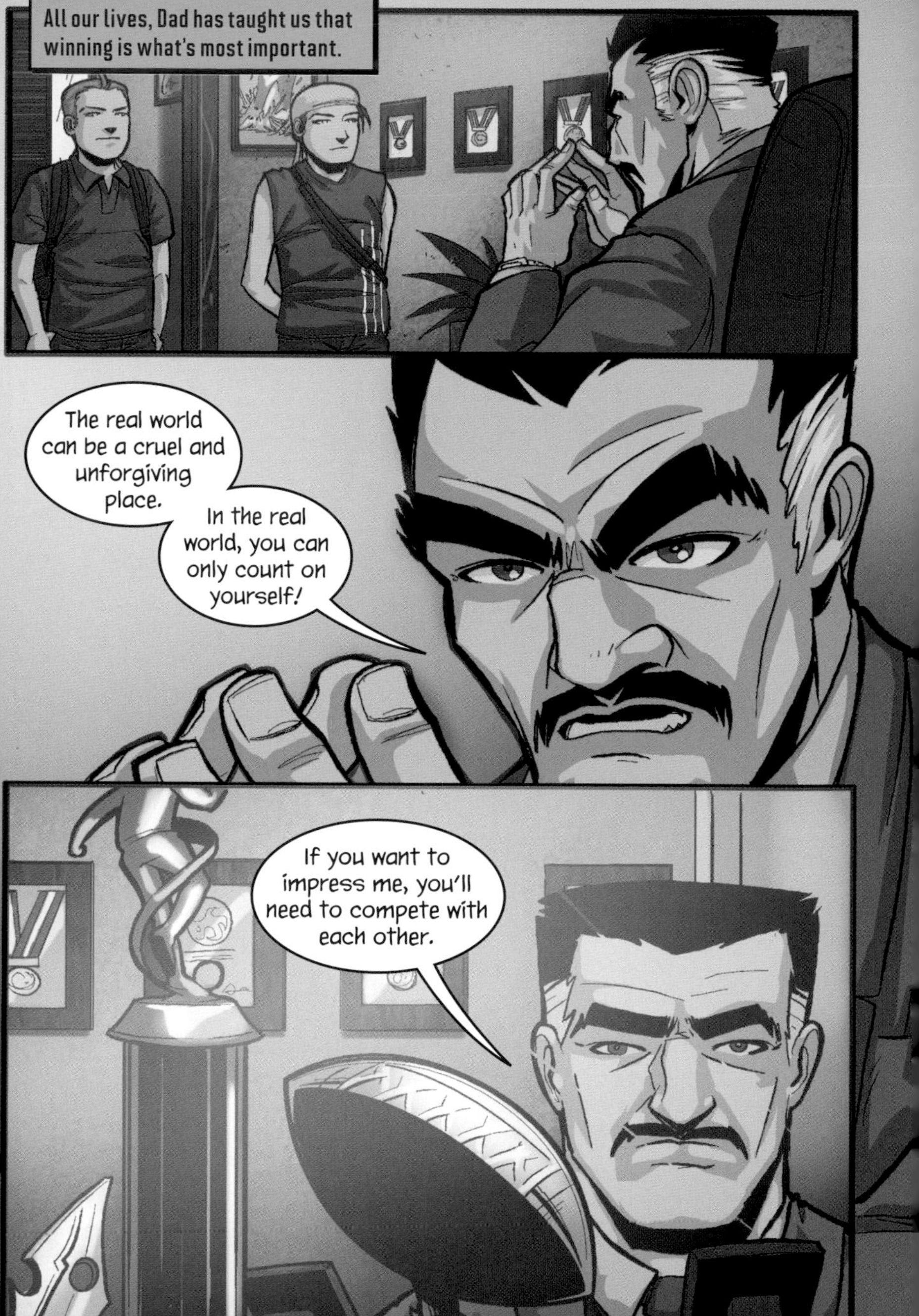

All our lives, Dad has taught us that winning is what's most important.
The real world can be a cruel and unforgiving place.
In the real world, you can only count on yourself!
If you want to impress me, you'll need to compete with each other.

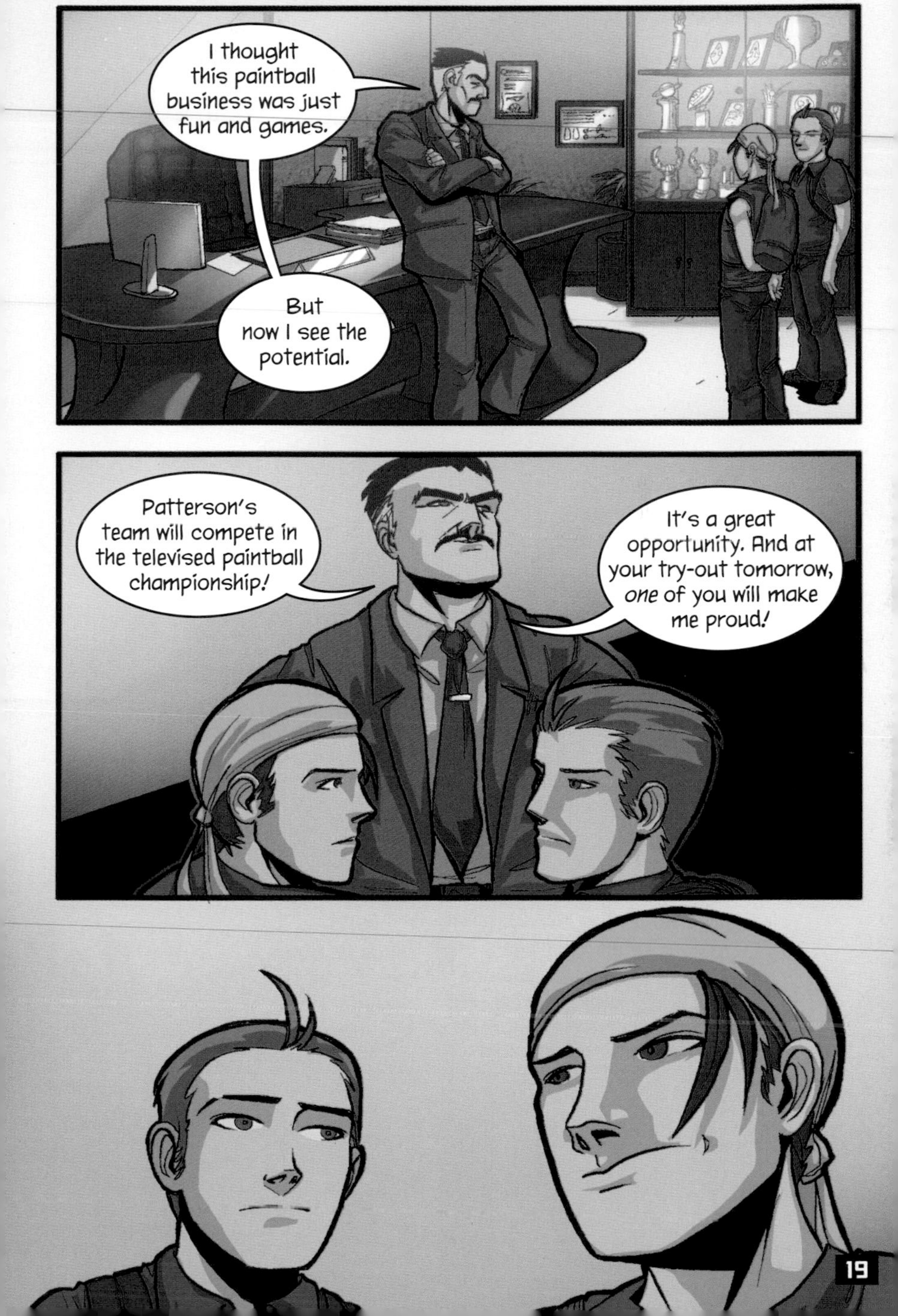
I thought this paintball business was just fun and games.
But now I see the potential.
Patterson's team will compete in the televised paintball championship!
It's a great opportunity. And at your try-out tomorrow, *one* of you will make me proud!

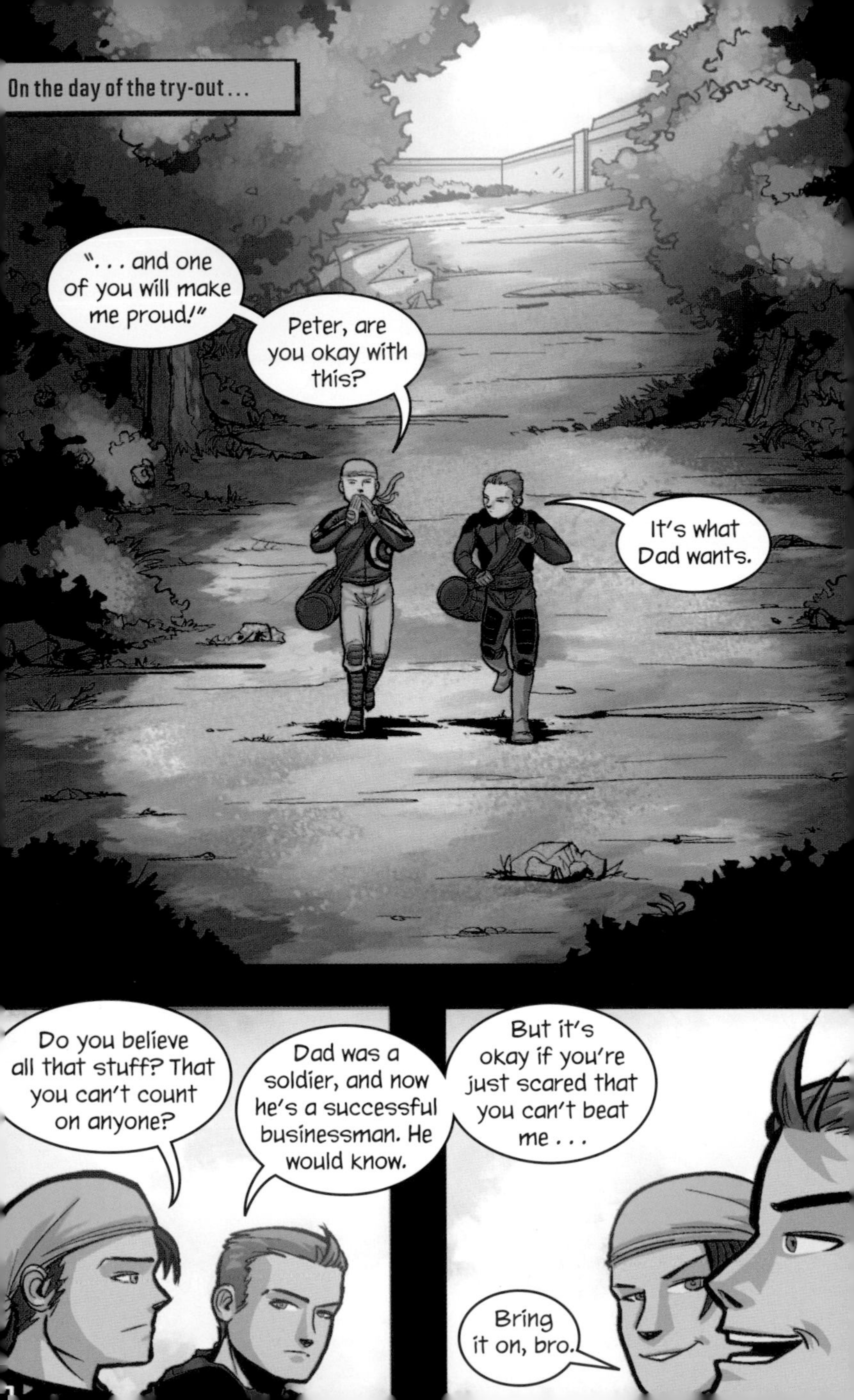
On the day of the try-out . . .
". . . and one of you will make me proud!"
Peter, are you okay with this?
It's what Dad wants.
Do you believe all that stuff? That you can't count on anyone?
Dad was a soldier, and now he's a successful businessman. He would know.
But it's okay if you're just scared that you can't beat me . . .
Bring it on, bro.

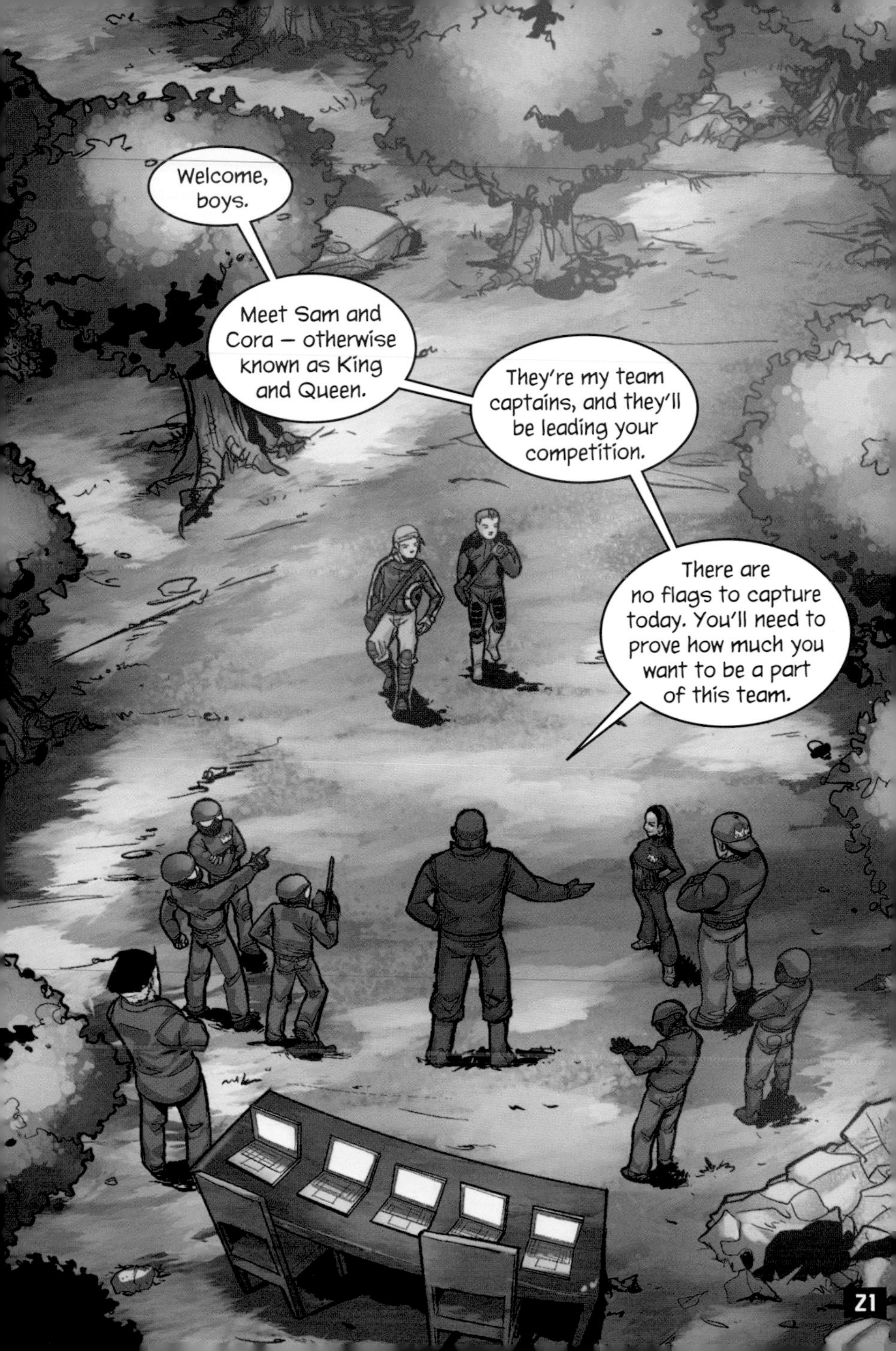
Welcome, boys.
Meet Sam and Cora – otherwise known as King and Queen.
They're my team captains, and they'll be leading your competition.
There are no flags to capture today. You'll need to prove how much you want to be a part of this team.

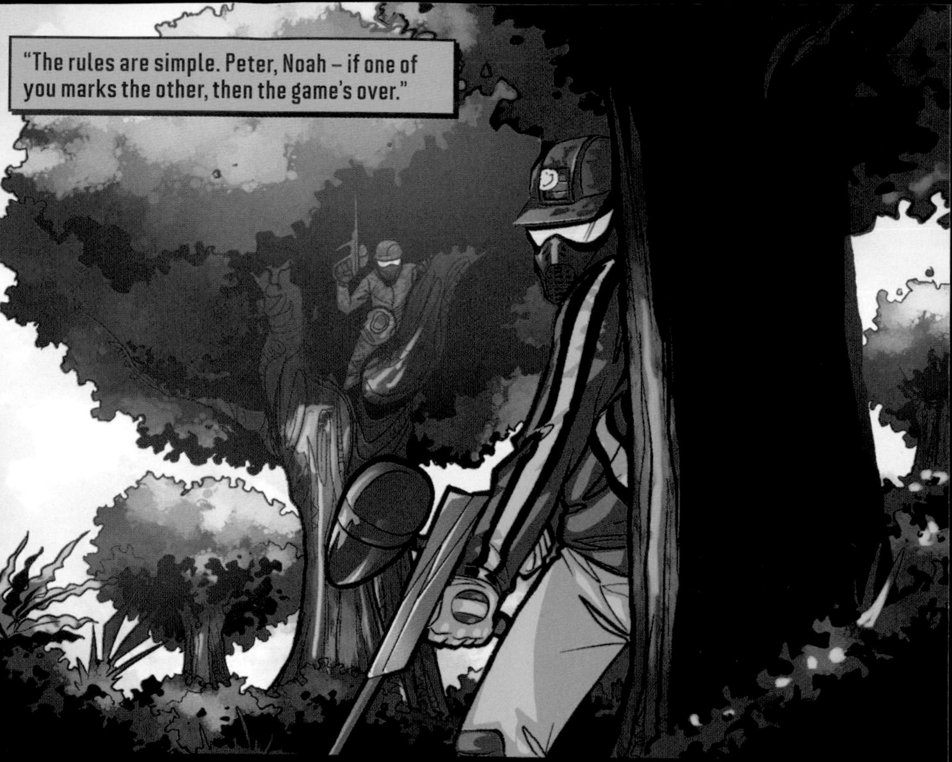
"The rules are simple. Peter, Noah – if one of you marks the other, then the game's over."

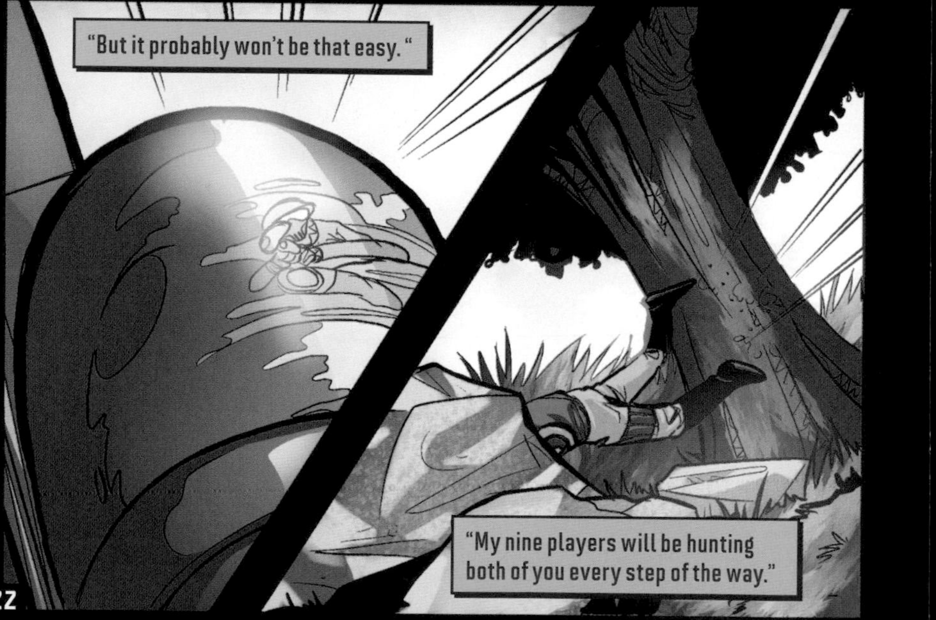
"But it probably won't be that easy. "
"My nine players will be hunting both of you every step of the way."

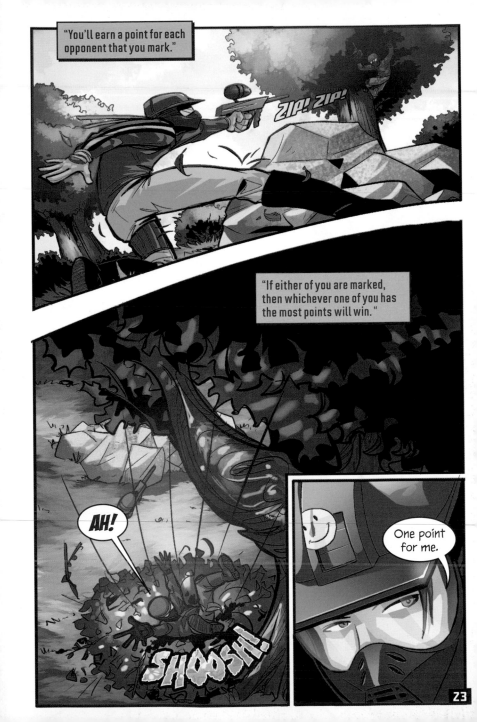

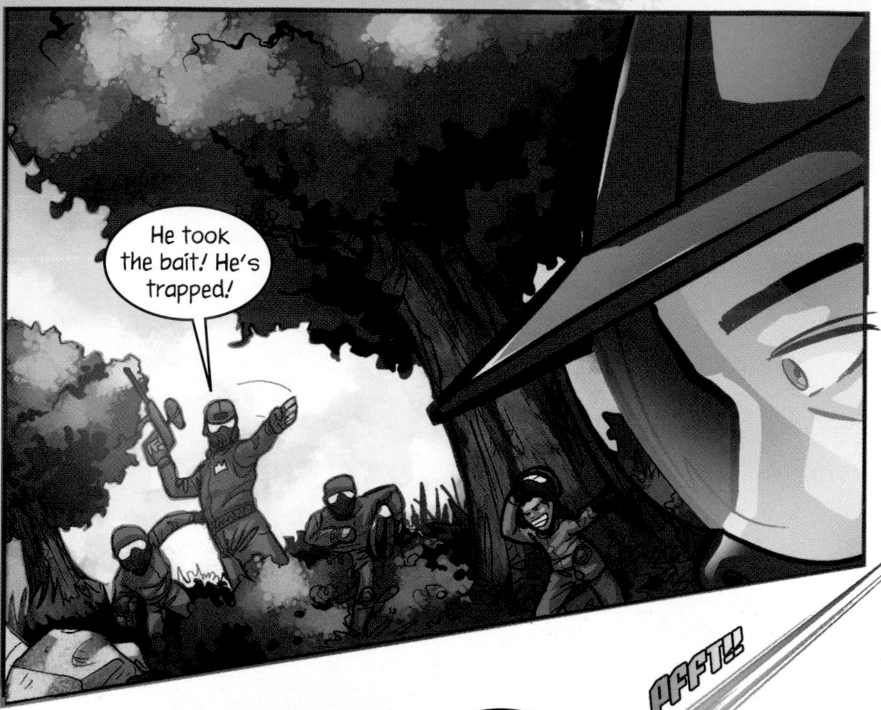
He took the bait! He's trapped!
PFFT!!
Uh-oh!
PFFT!!
PFFT!!
PFFT!!
PFFT!!
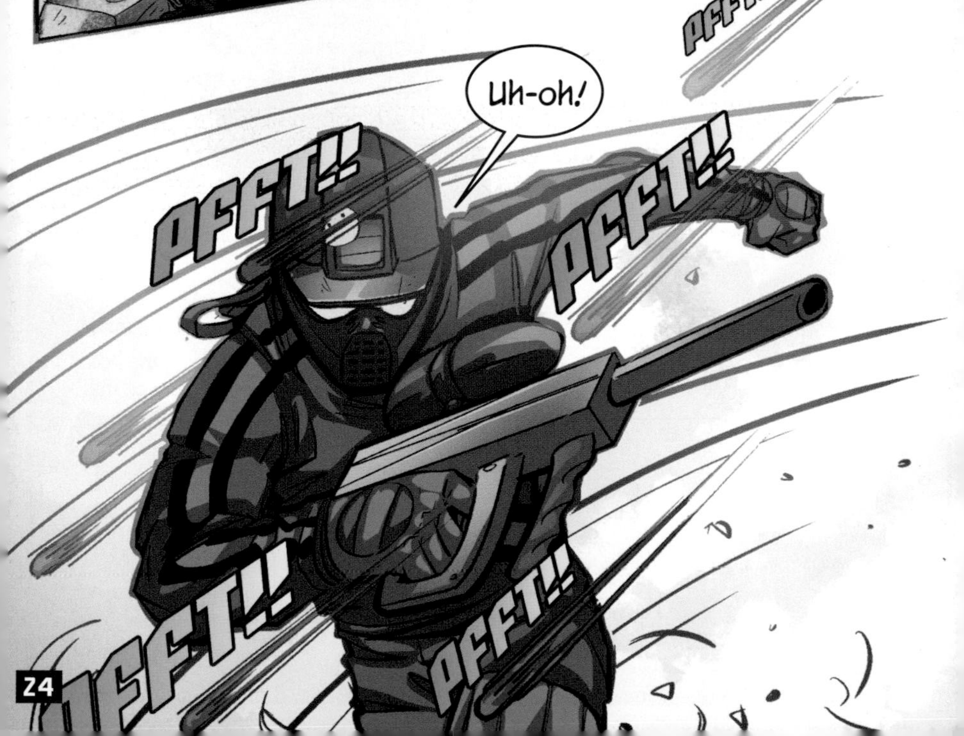

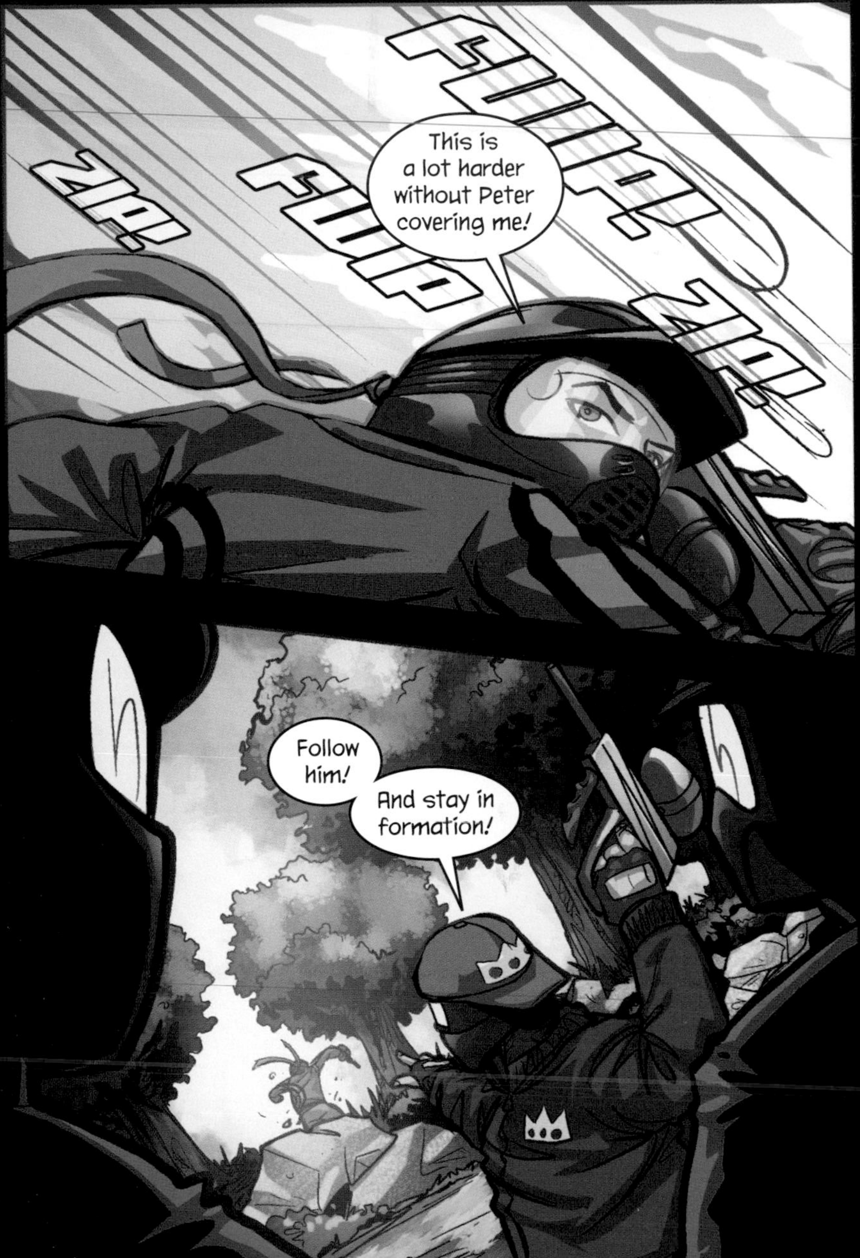
ZIP!
FUUP
FUUP!
ZIP!
This is a lot harder without Peter covering me!
Follow him!
And stay in formation!

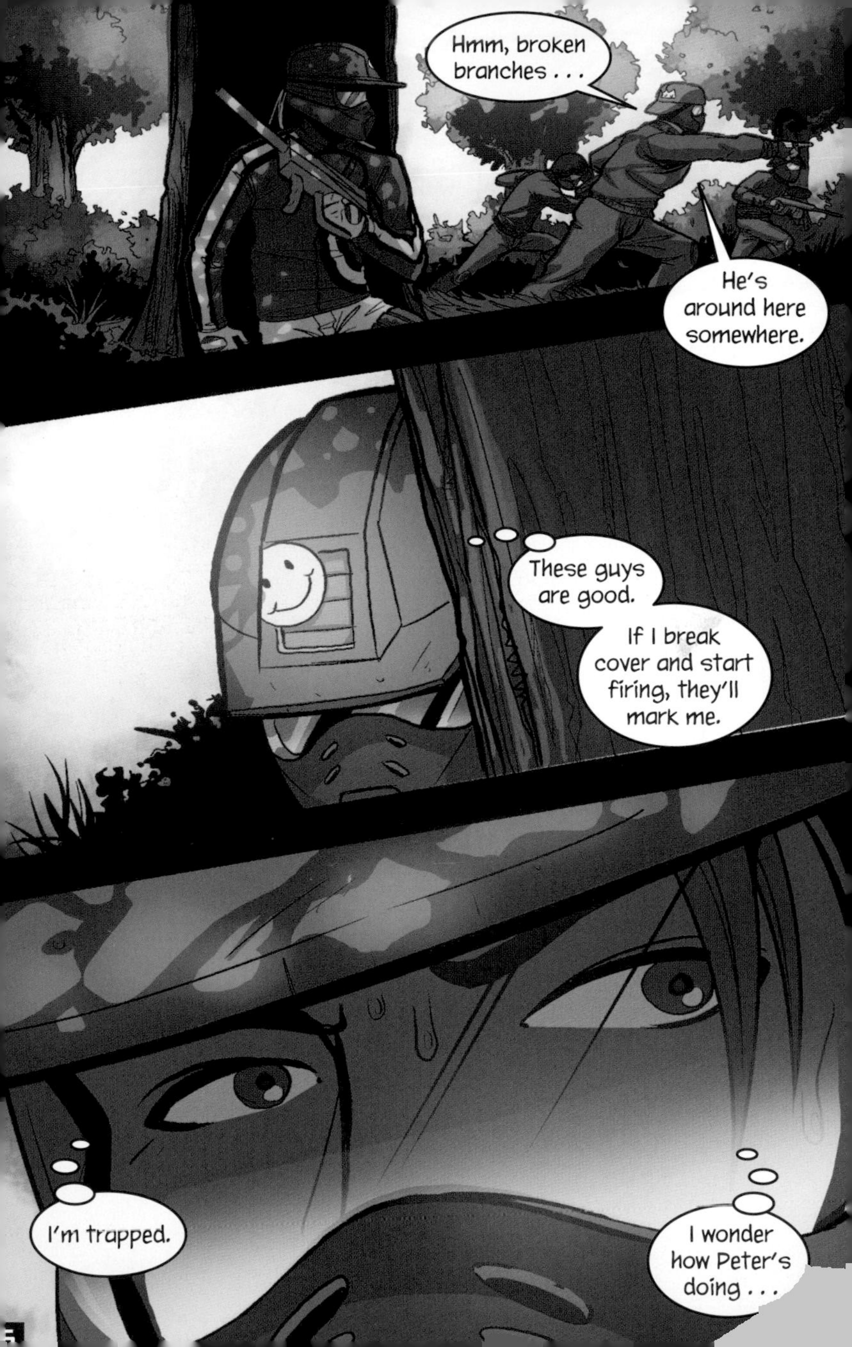
Hmm, broken branches . . .
He's around here somewhere.
These guys are good.
If I break cover and start firing, they'll mark me.
I'm trapped.
I wonder how Peter's doing . . .

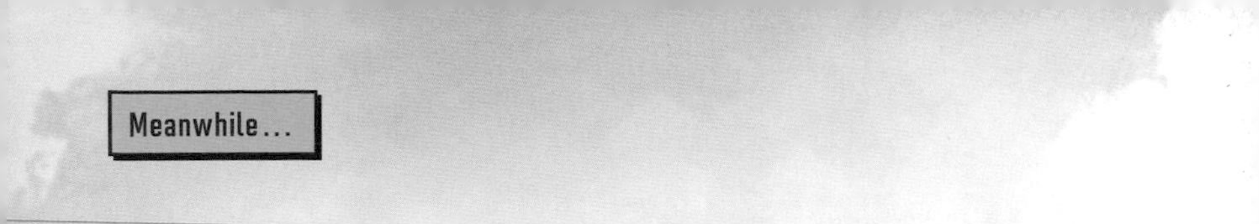
Meanwhile...

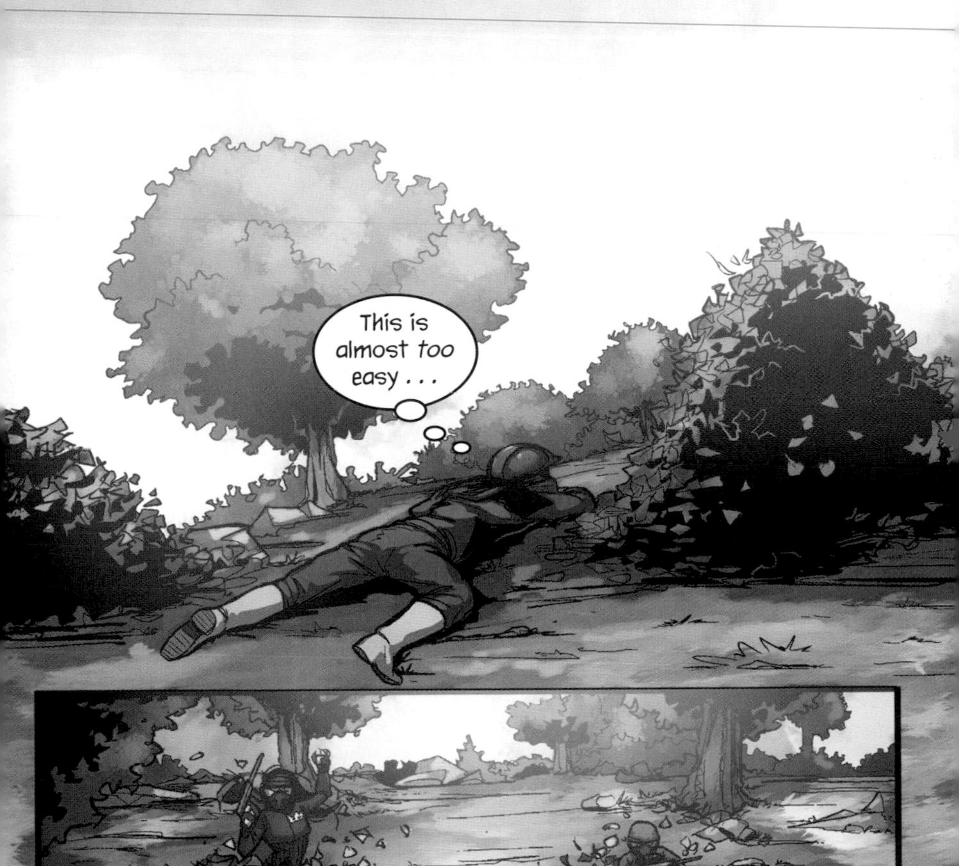
This is almost too easy . . .

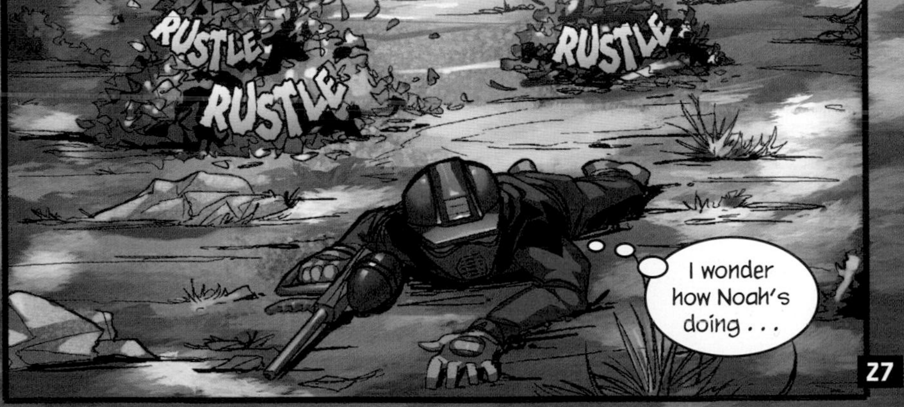
RUSTLE
RUSTLE
RUSTLE
I wonder how Noah's doing . . .

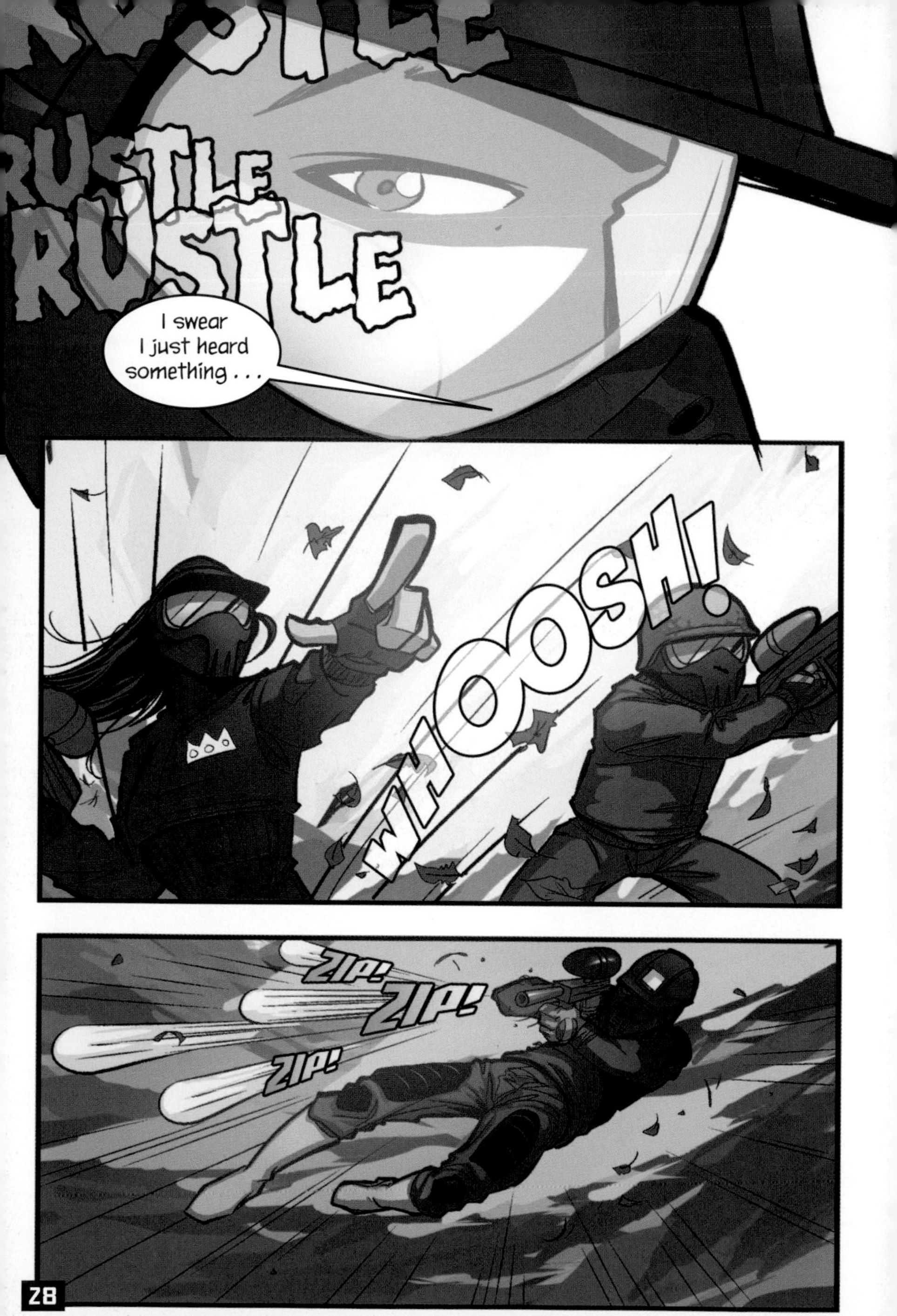
RUSTLE
RUSTLE
RUSTLE
I swear I just heard something . . .
WHOOSH!
ZIP!
ZIP!
ZIP!

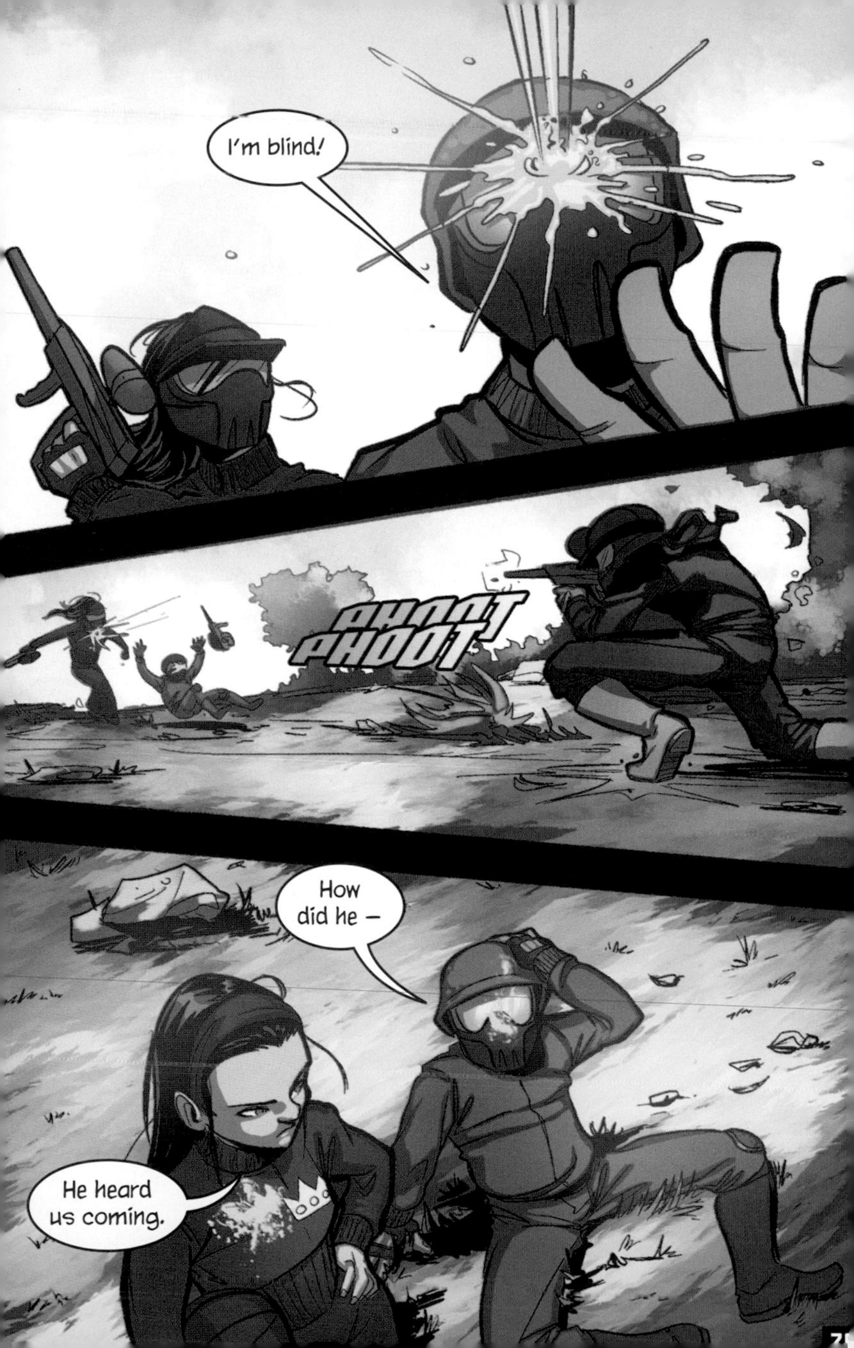
I'm blind!
PHOOT PHOOT
How did he –
He heard us coming.

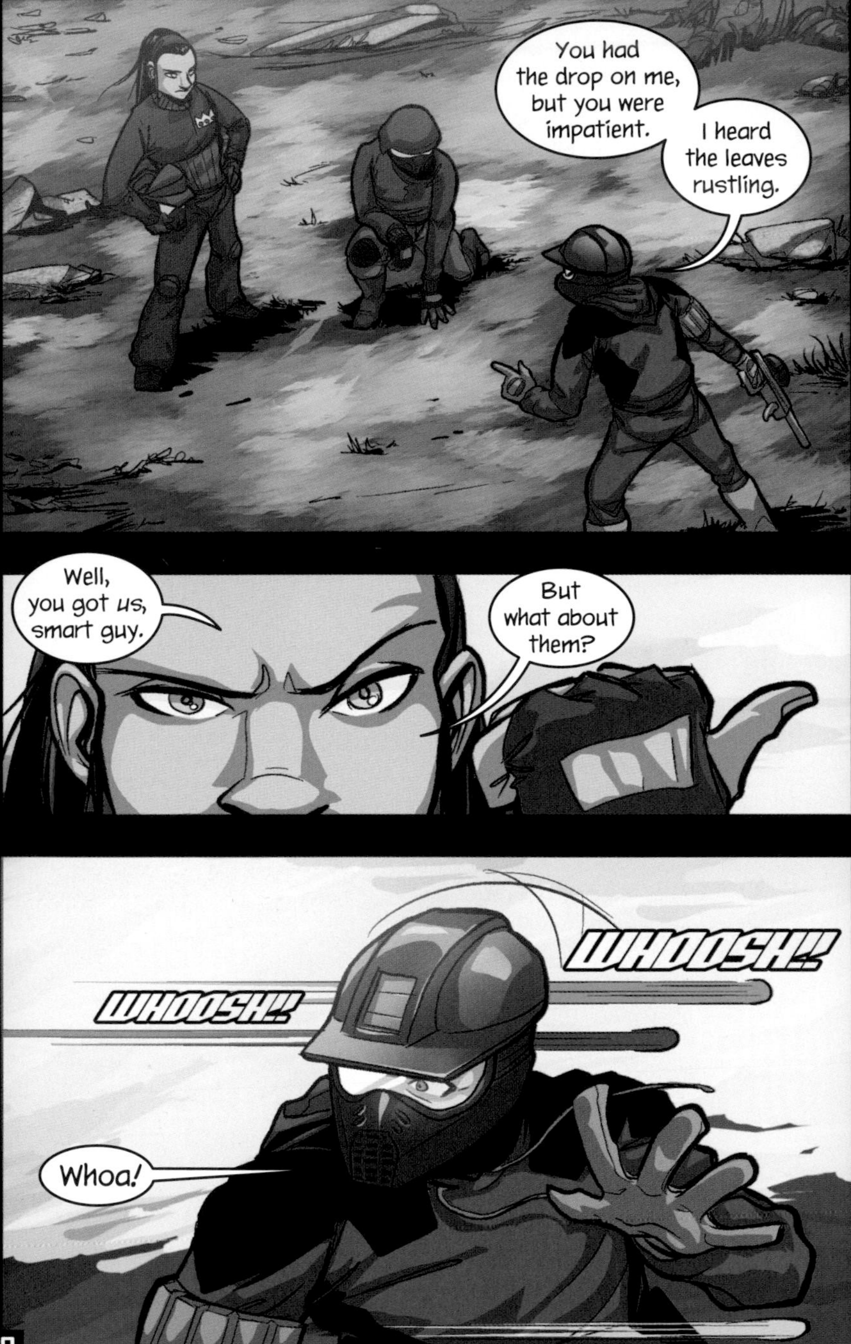
You had the drop on me, but you were impatient.
I heard the leaves rustling.
Well, you got us, smart guy.
But what about them?
WHOOSH!!
WHOOSH!!
Whoa!

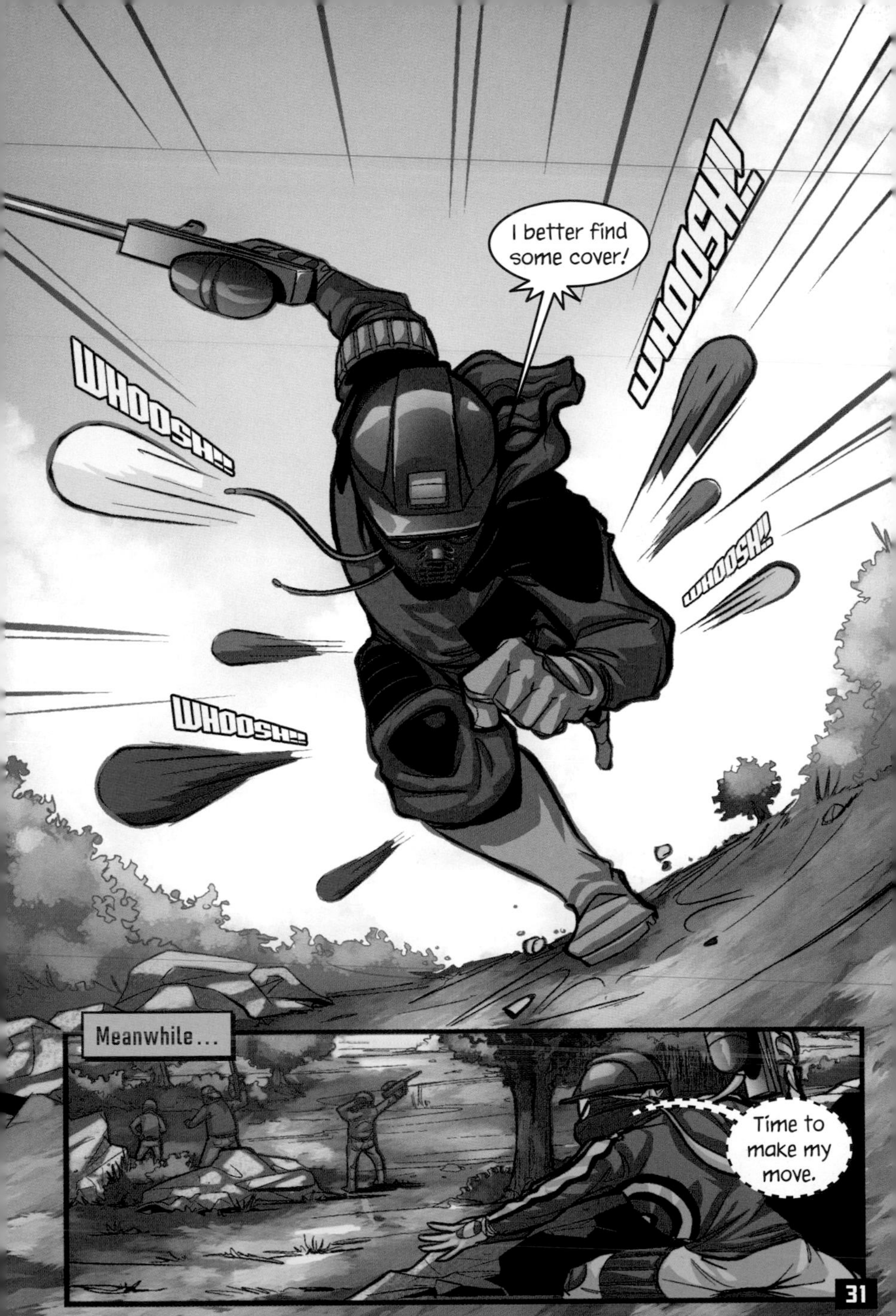
I better find some cover!
WHOOSH!!
WHOOSH!!
WHOOSH!!
WHOOSH!!
Meanwhile . . .
Time to make my move.

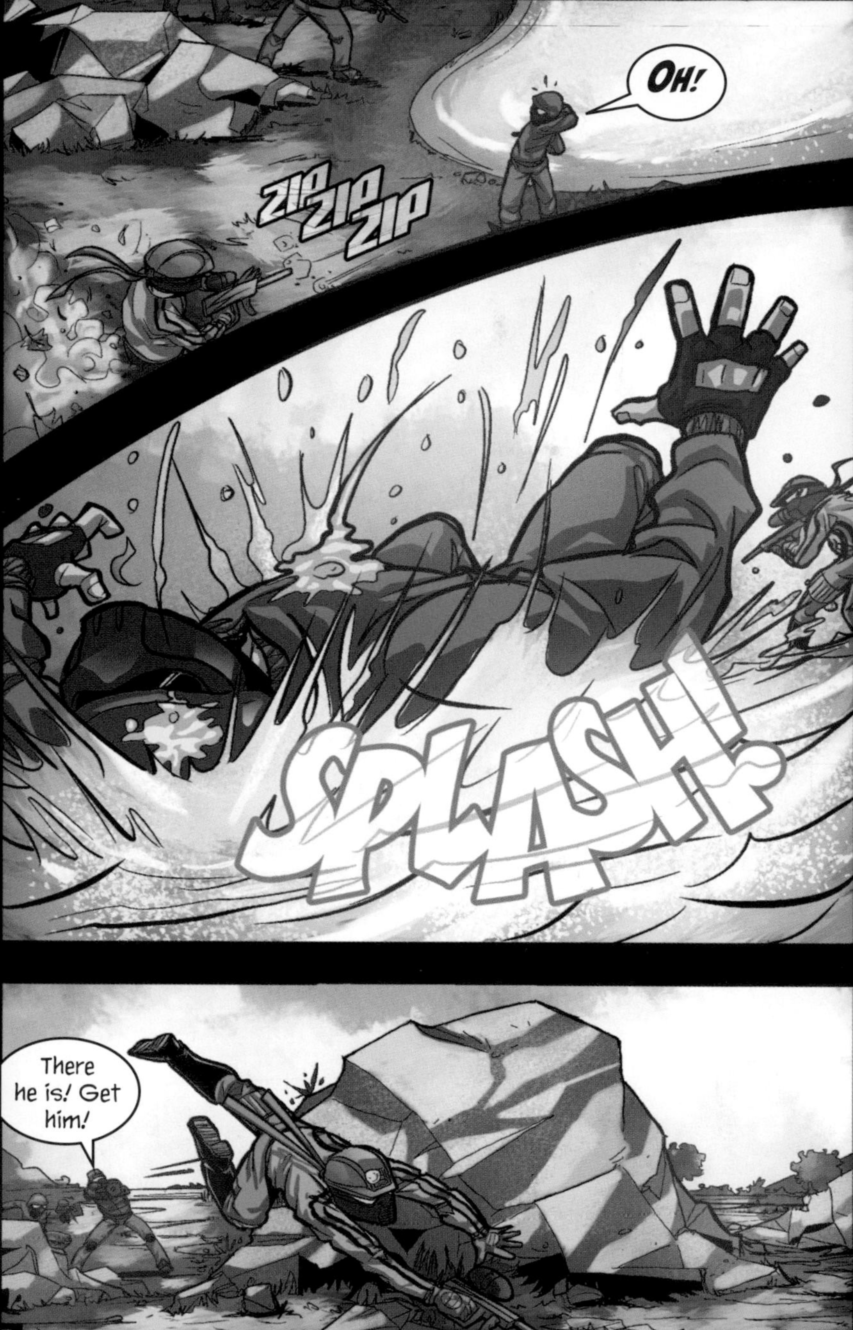
OH!
ZIP ZIP ZIP
SPLASH!
There he is! Get him!

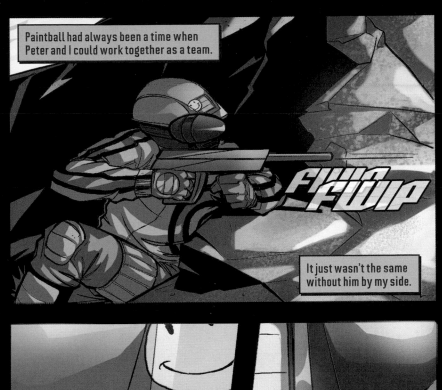

Paintball had always been a time when Peter and I could work together as a team.

FWIP FWIP

It just wasn't the same without him by my side.

But maybe Dad is right.

Maybe winning is what's most important.

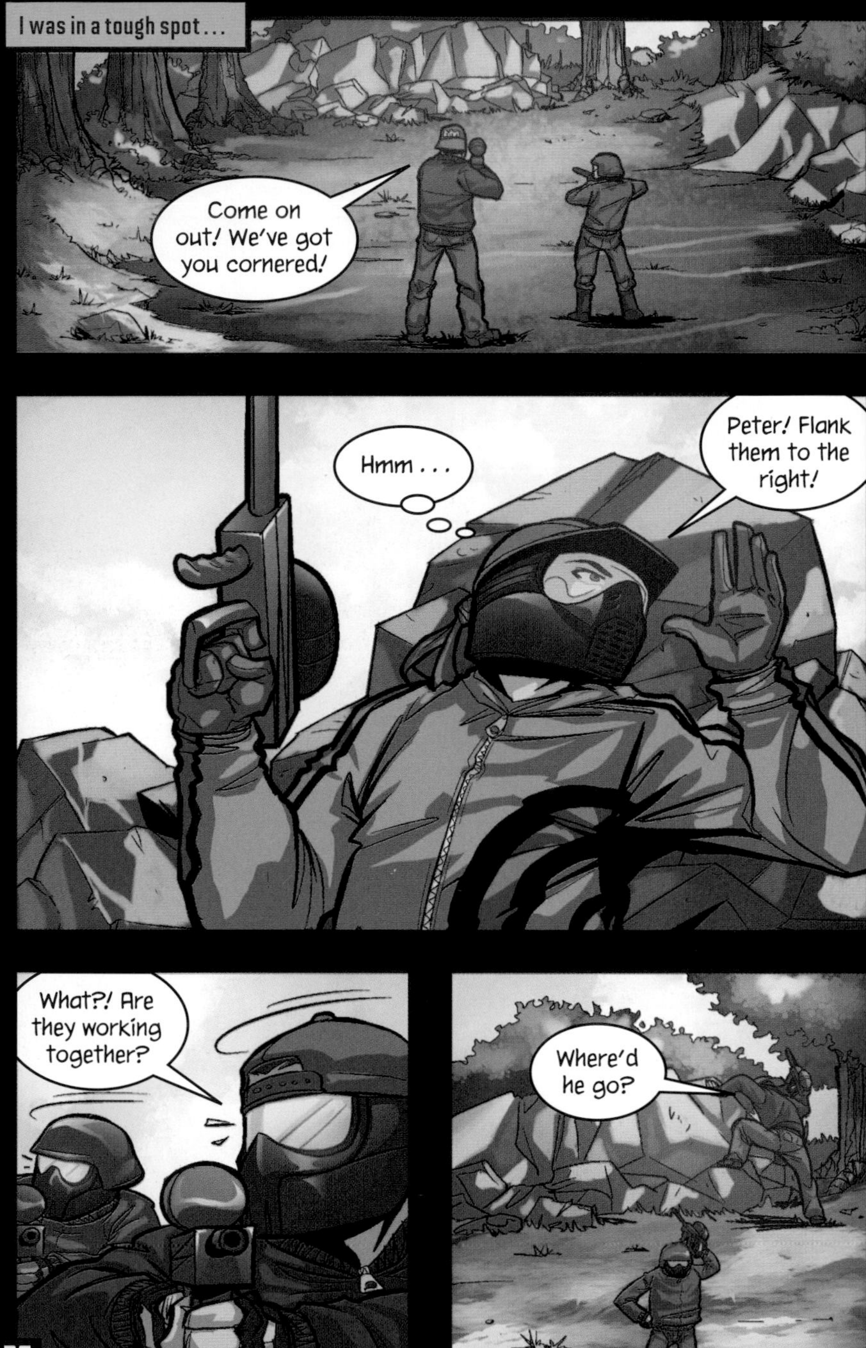
I was in a tough spot . . .
Come on out! We've got you cornered!
Hmm . . .
Peter! Flank them to the right!
What?! Are they working together?
Where'd he go?

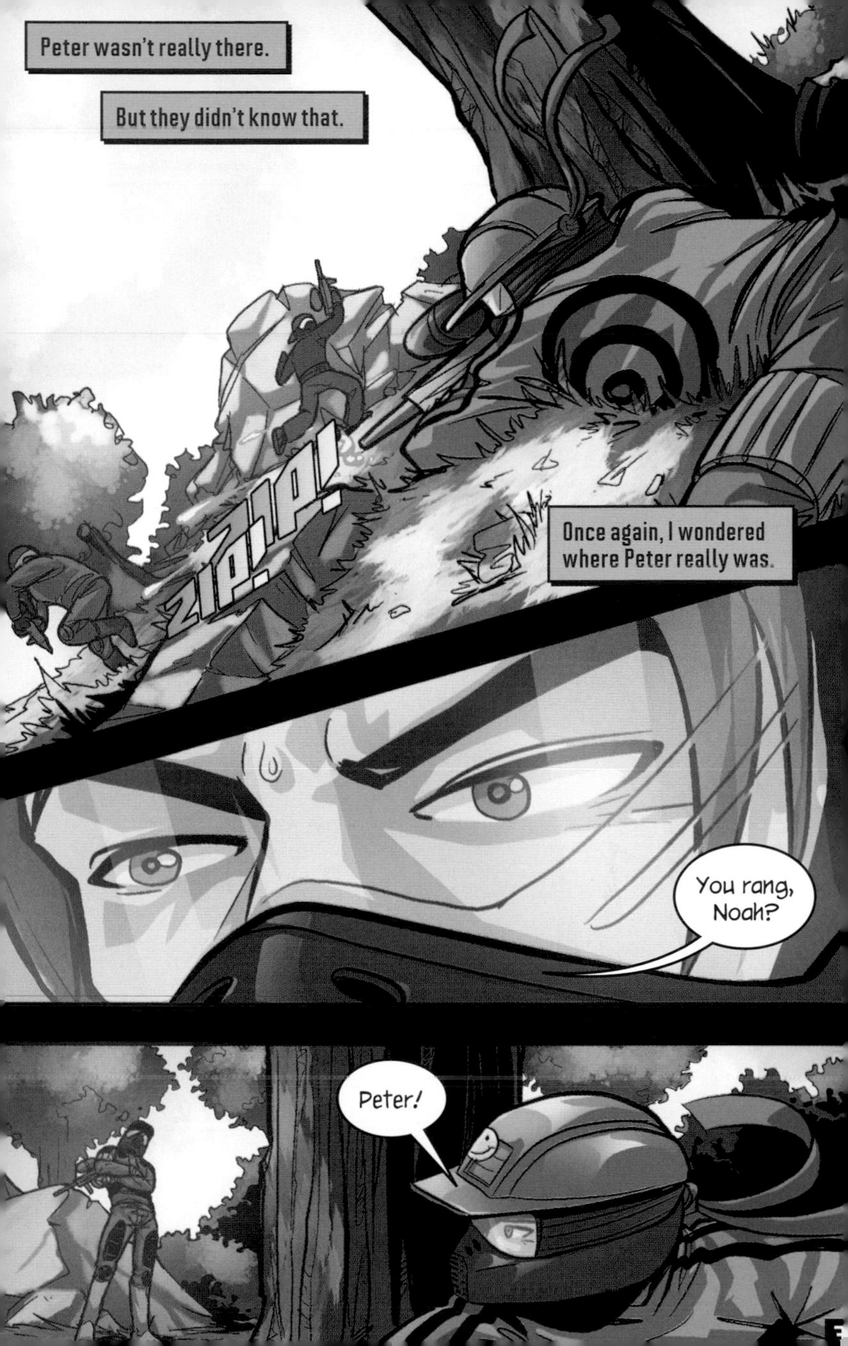
Peter wasn't really there.
But they didn't know that.
ZIP! ZIP! ZIP!
Once again, I wondered where Peter really was.
You rang, Noah?
Peter!

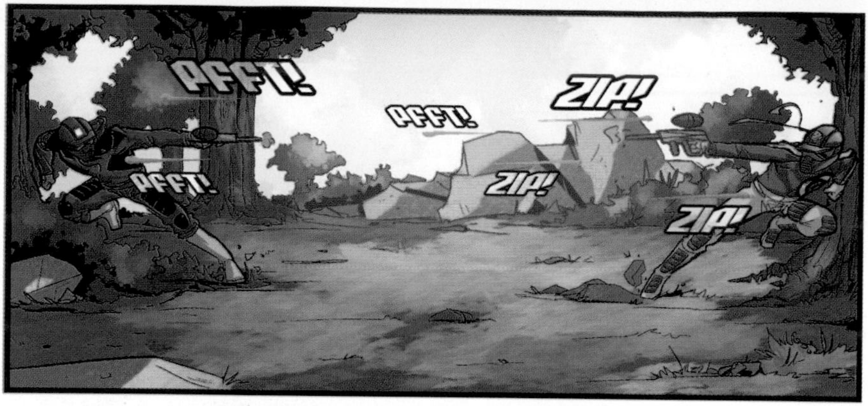

PFFT!
PFFT!
PFFT!
ZIP!
ZIP!
ZIP!

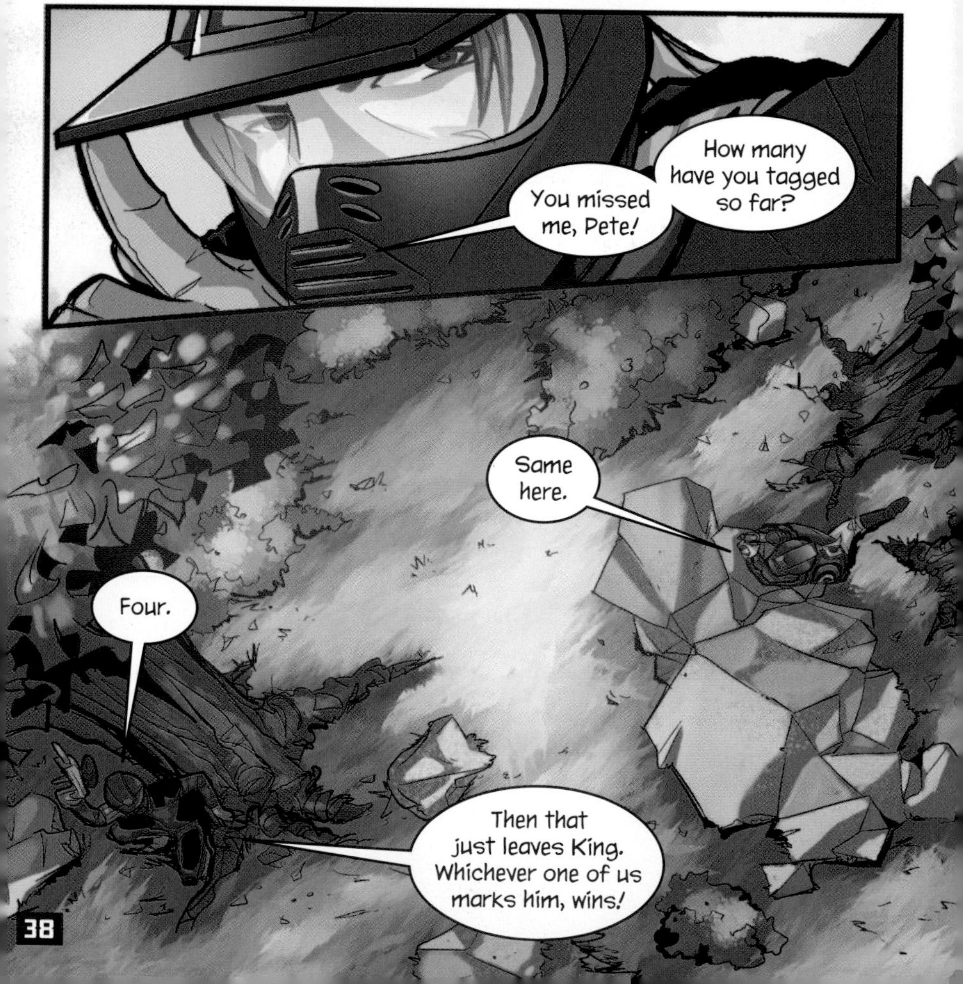

You missed me, Pete!
How many have you tagged so far?
Same here.
Four.
Then that just leaves King. Whichever one of us marks him, wins!

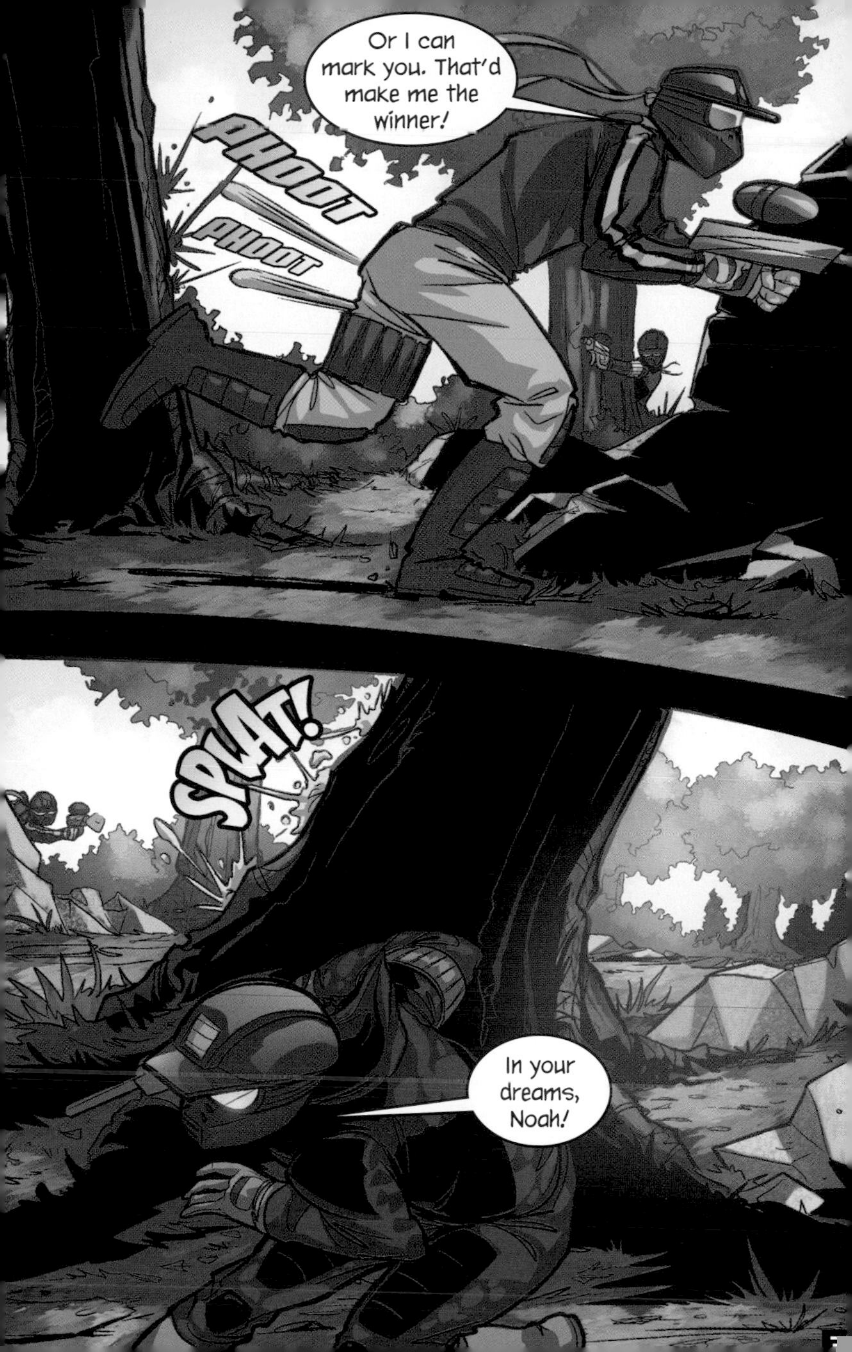
Or I can mark you. That'd make me the winner!
PHOOT
PHOOT
SPLAT!
In your dreams, Noah!

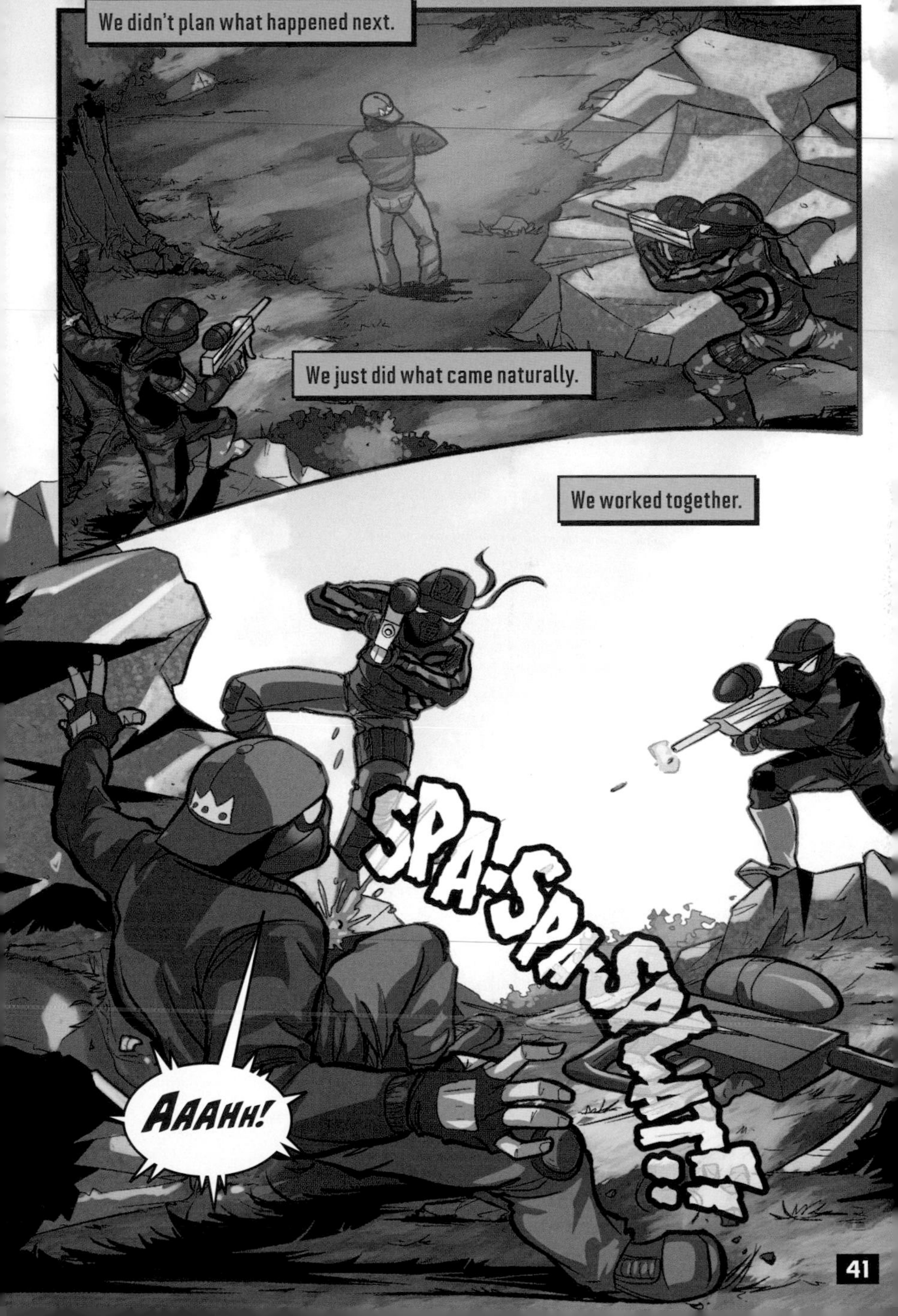
We didn't plan what happened next.
We just did what came naturally.
We worked together.
SPA-SPA-SPLAT!!
AAAHH!

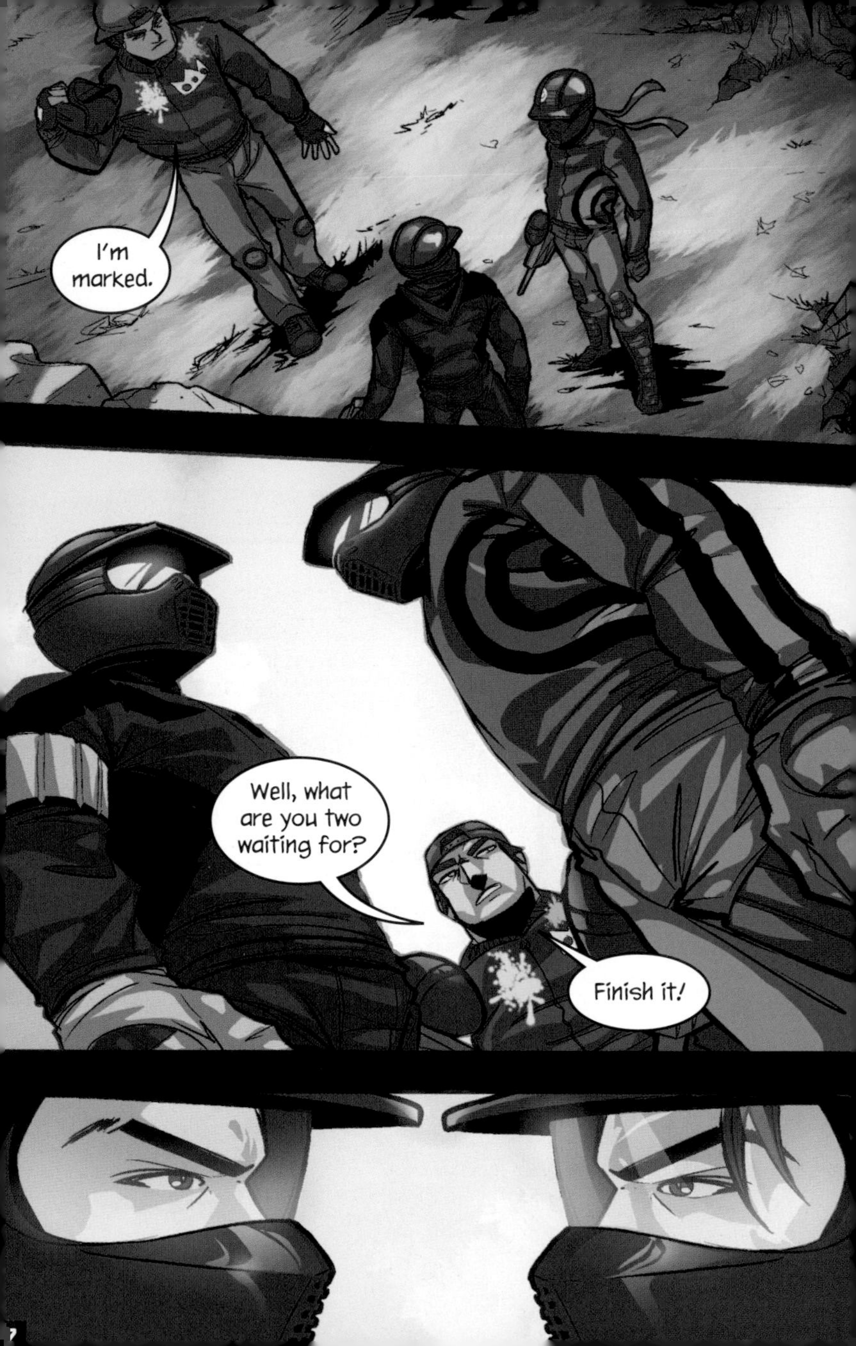
I'm marked.
Well, what are you two waiting for?
Finish it!

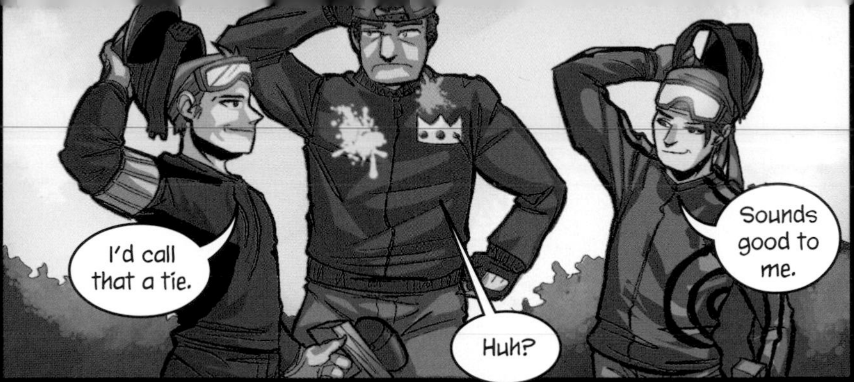
I'd call that a tie.
Huh?
Sounds good to me.

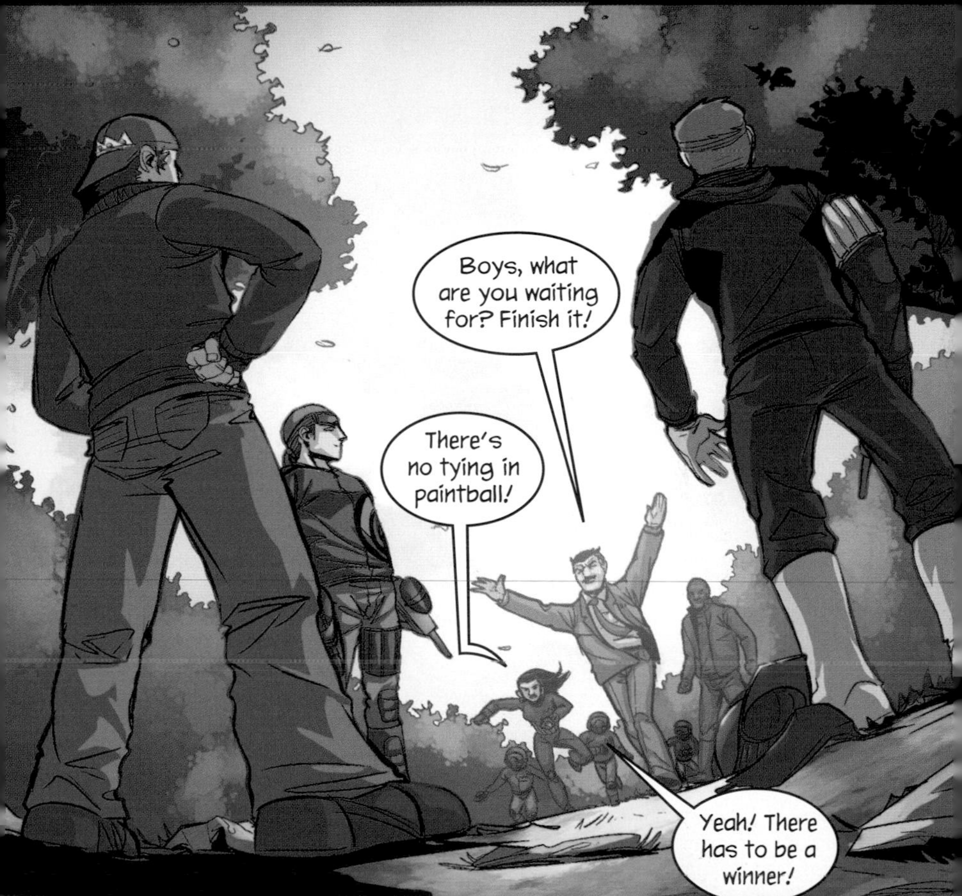
Boys, what are you waiting for? Finish it!
There's no tying in paintball!
Yeah! There has to be a winner!

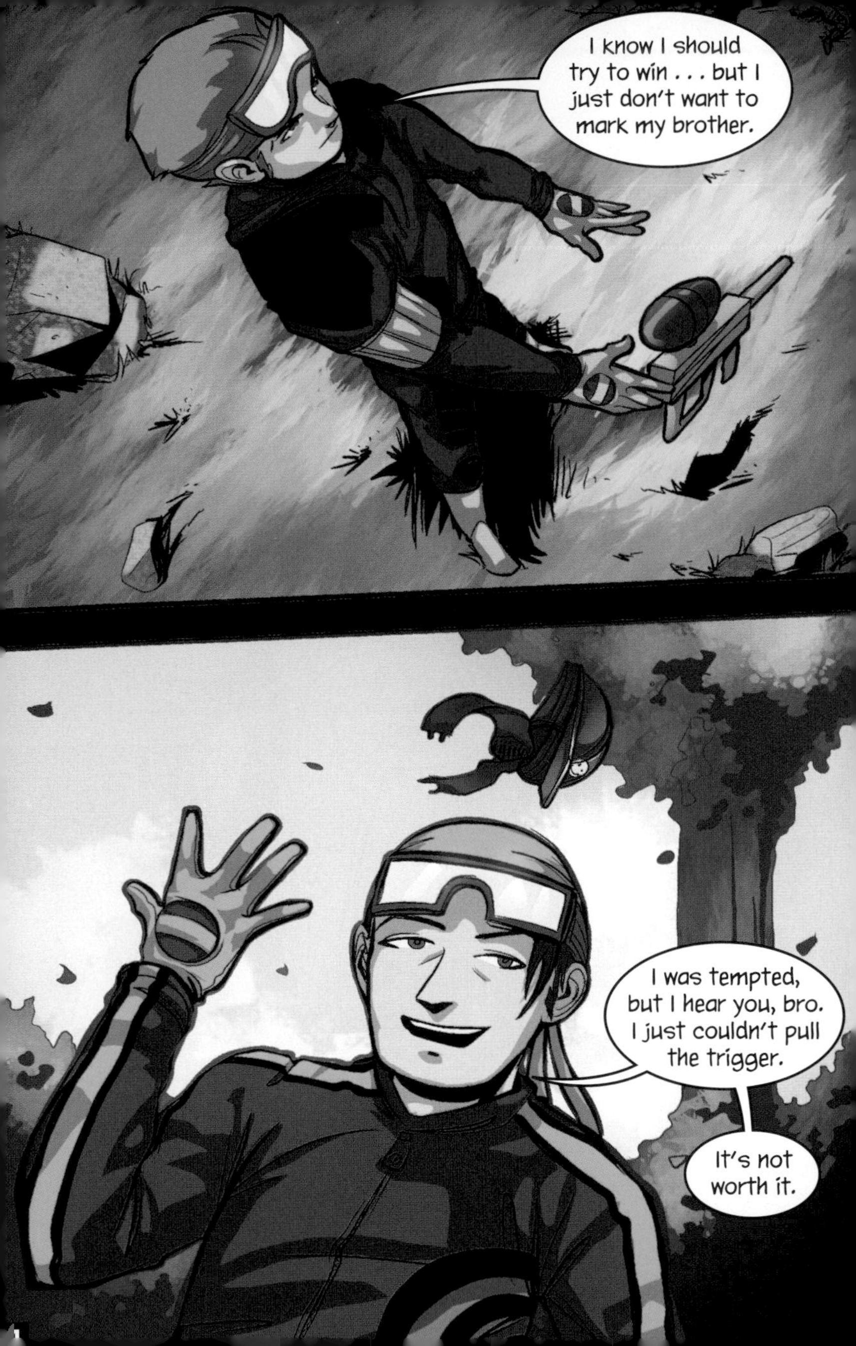
I know I should try to win . . . but I just don't want to mark my brother.
I was tempted, but I hear you, bro. I just couldn't pull the trigger.
It's not worth it.

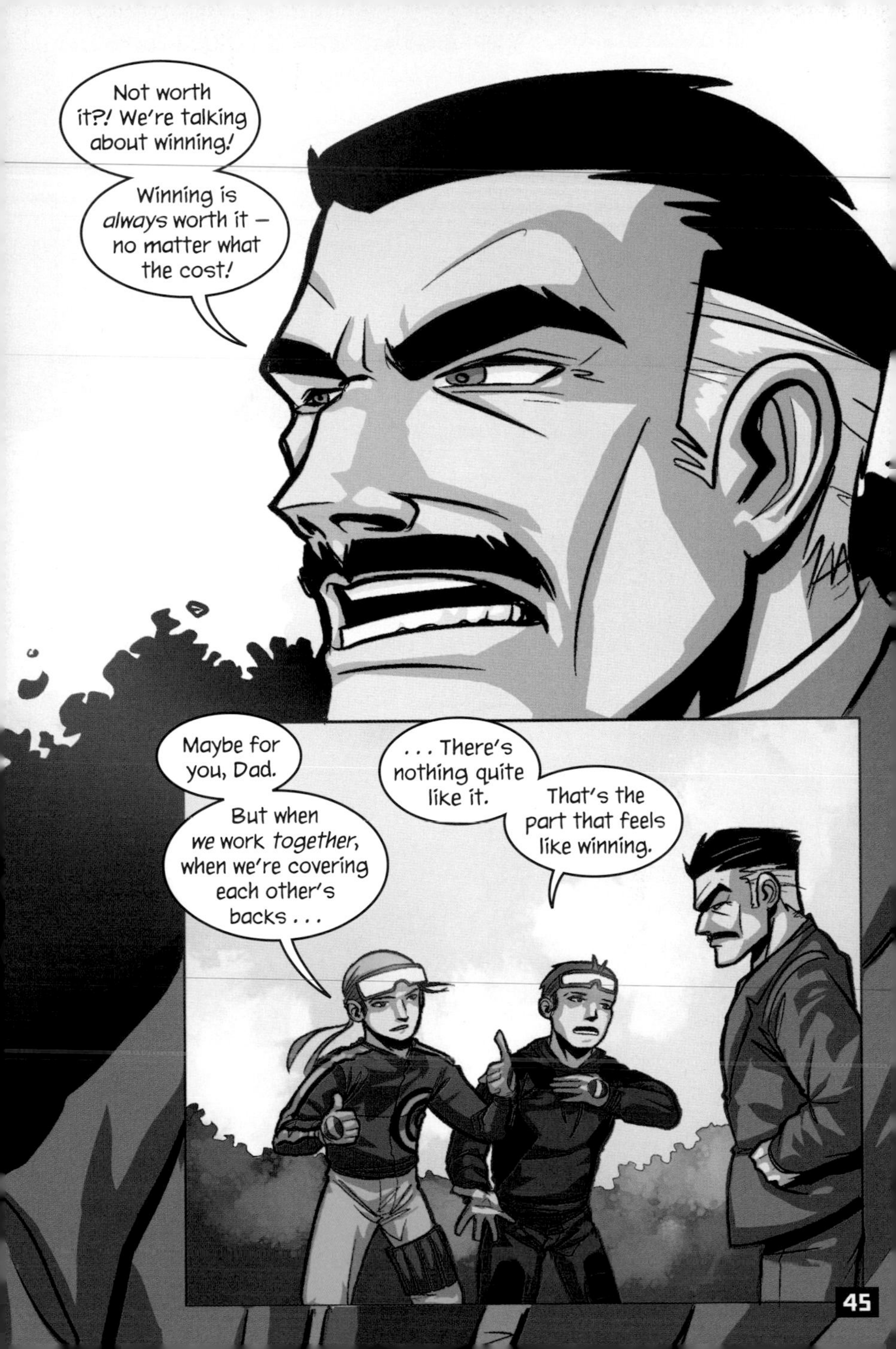
Not worth it?! We're talking about winning!
Winning is *always* worth it — no matter what the cost!
Maybe for you, Dad.
But when *we* work *together*, when we're covering each other's backs . . .
. . . There's nothing quite like it.
That's the part that feels like winning.

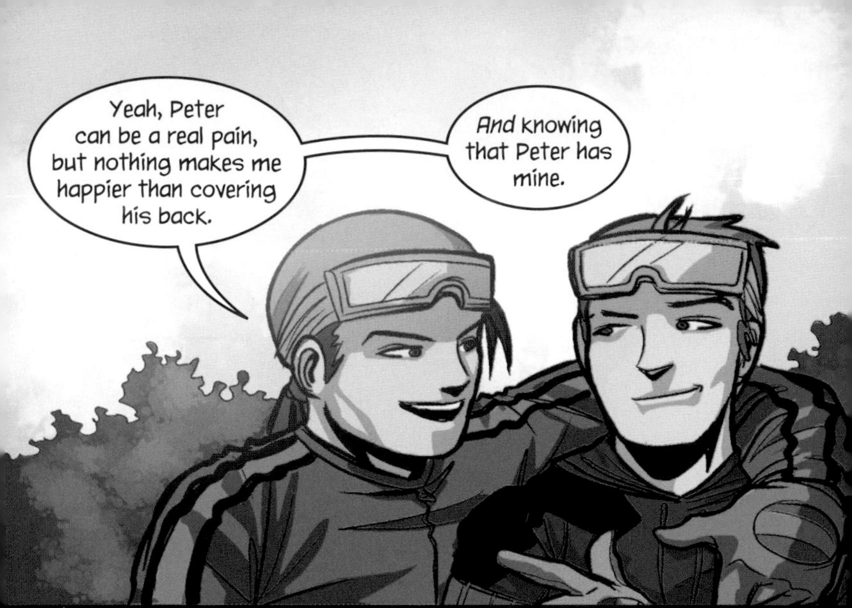
Yeah, Peter can be a real pain, but nothing makes me happier than covering his back.
And knowing that Peter has mine.

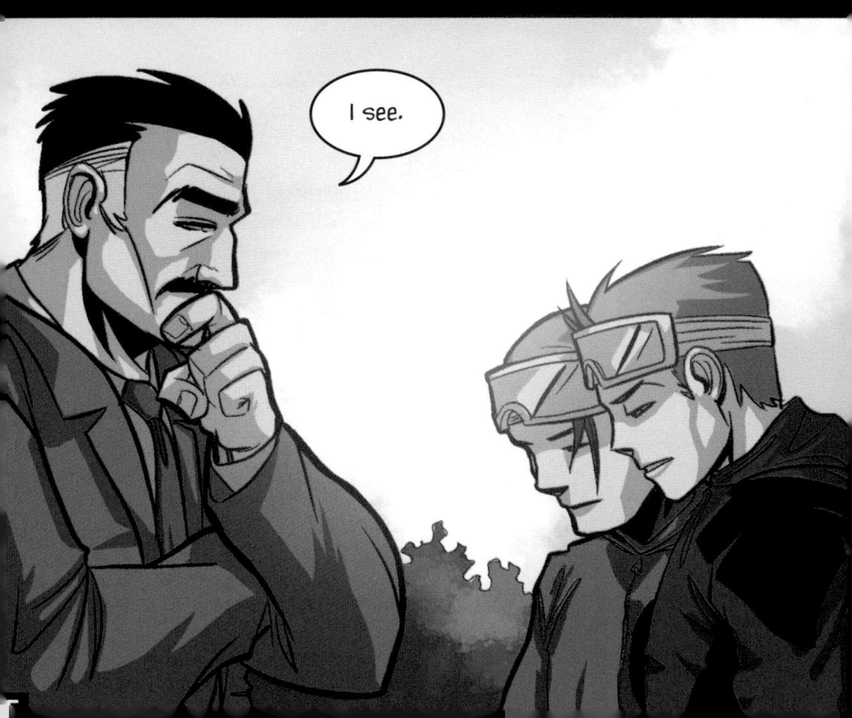
I see.

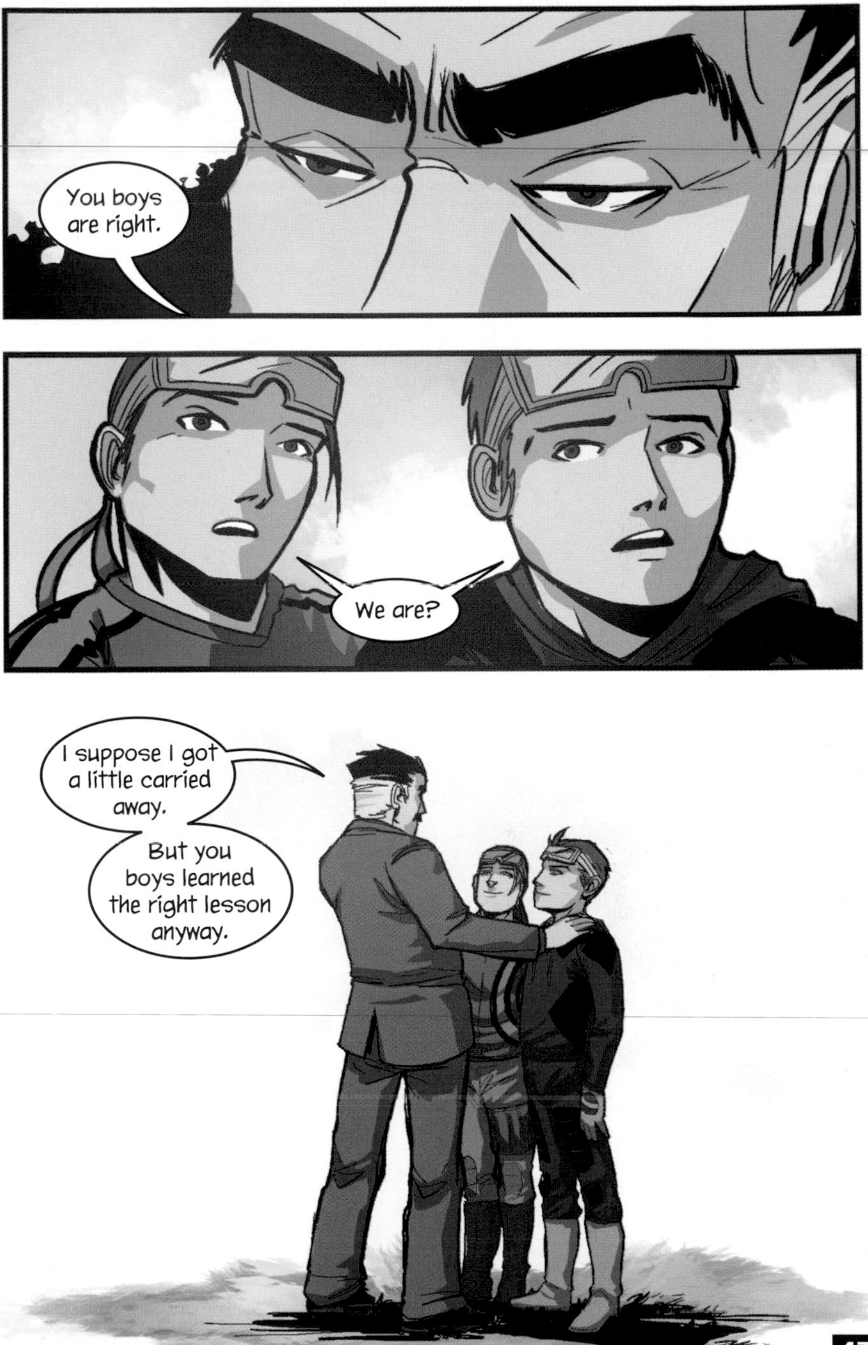
You boys are right.
We are?
I suppose I got a little carried away.
But you boys learned the right lesson anyway.

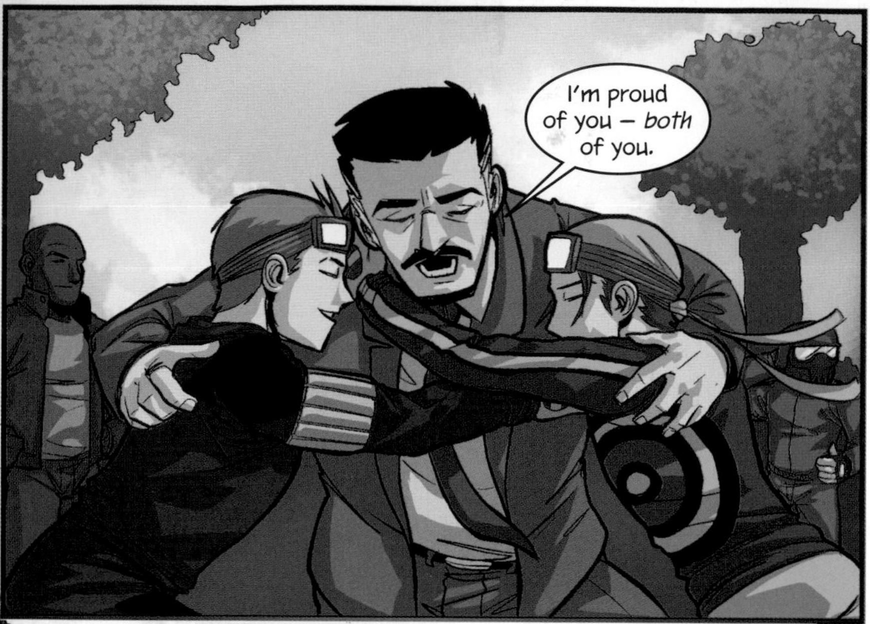
I'm proud of you – *both* of you.

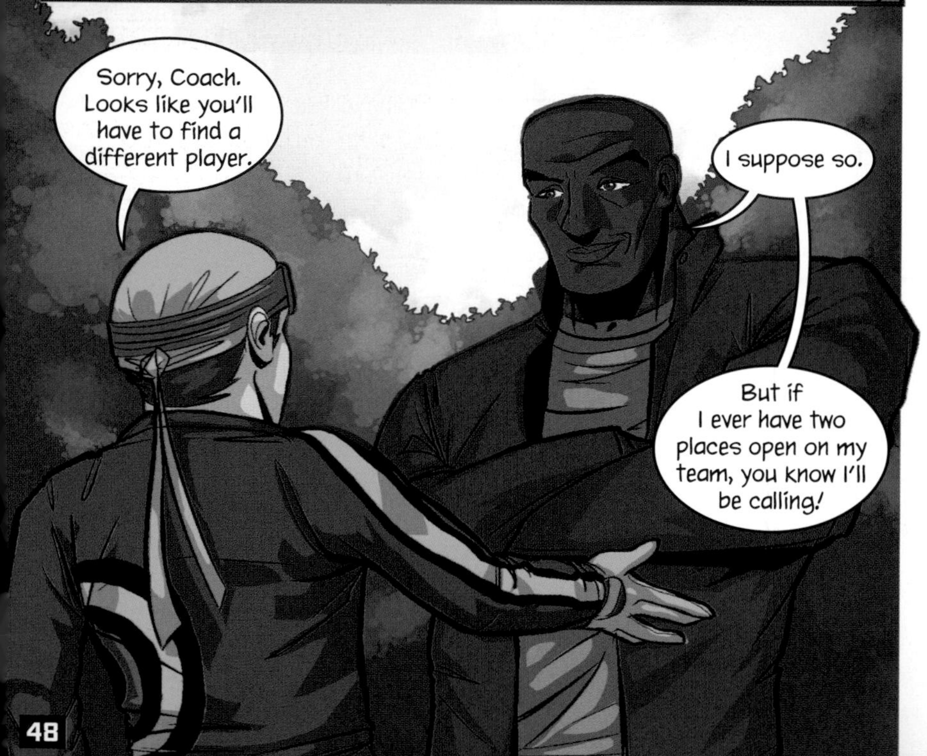
Sorry, Coach. Looks like you'll have to find a different player.
I suppose so.
But if I ever have two places open on my team, you know I'll be calling!

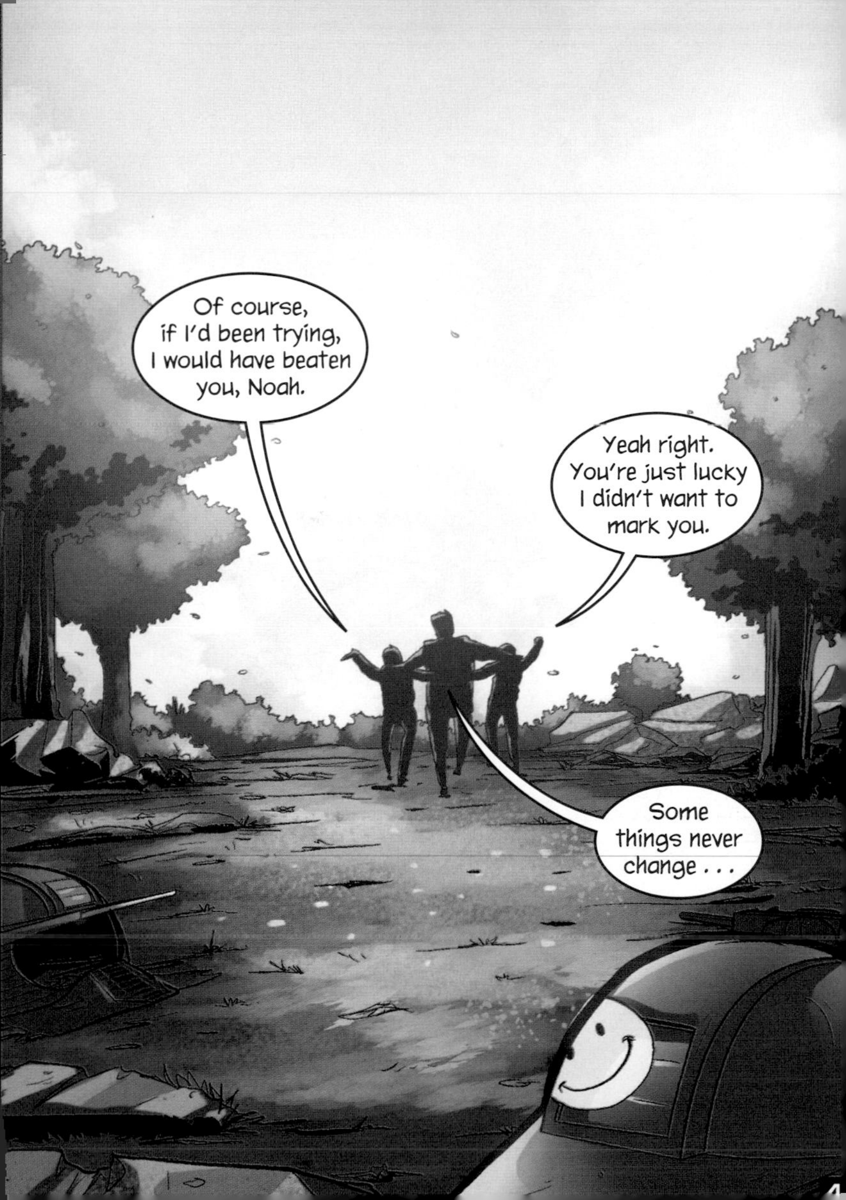
Of course, if I'd been trying, I would have beaten you, Noah.
Yeah right. You're just lucky I didn't want to mark you.
Some things never change . . .

SPORTS ZONE

POSTGAME RECAP

PNT PAINTBALL

FBL FOOTBALL

SKT SKATEBOARDING

BSL BASEBALL

BBL BASKETBALL

HKY HOCKEY

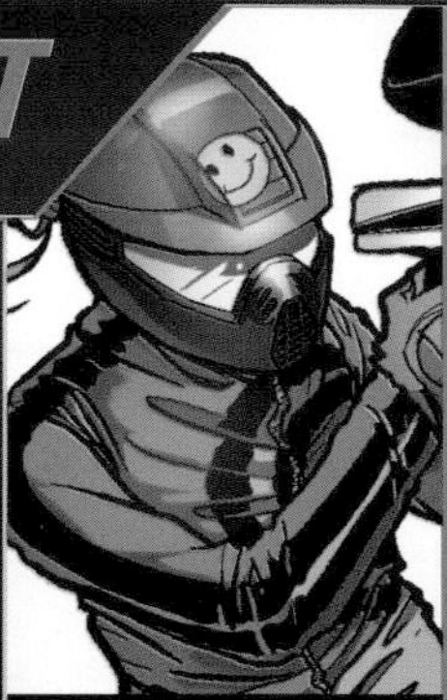

NOAH

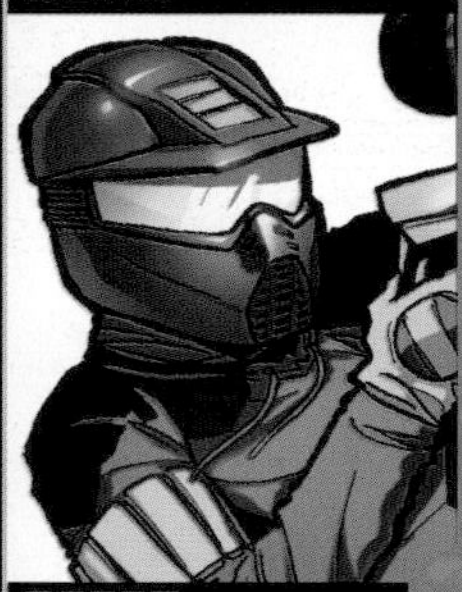

PETER

ECCLESTON TWINS LAY DOWN THEIR MARKERS AND CALL IT A DRAW!

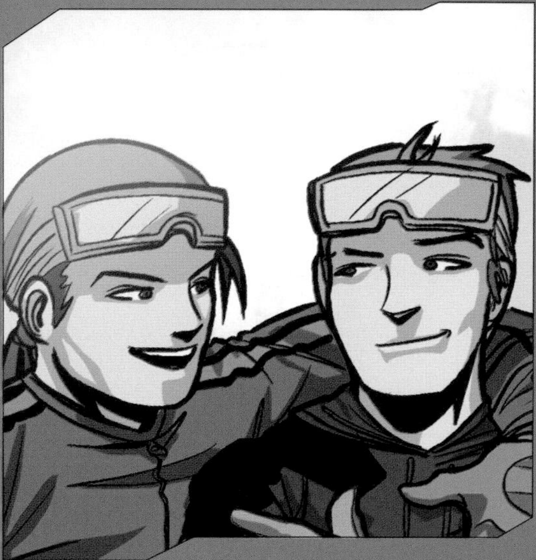

BY THE NUMBERS

FINAL SCORE:
DRAW

POINTS:
NOAH: 5 MARKS
PETER: 5 MARKS

STORY: The heated sibling rivalry in the Royals team try-out came to an unexpected conclusion when both twins readied their markers, took aim, and . . . laid down their arms! The shocking tie forces the Royals to look elsewhere for a new player. Coach Patterson was quoted as saying, “I’m disappointed that one of the Eccleston twins won’t be joining our squad, but I’m impressed by their show of brotherhood.”

Sports Illustrated KIDS

UP NEXT: SI KIDS INFO CENTRE

BLZ vs BKS
3-1
TGR vs ROR
33-32
EAG vs BAN
14-7
SPA vs WLD
4-3
BAN vs ROR
21-15
RZR vs LIG
4-3
BLZ vs BKS

Today, paintball fans got to see an amazing, action-packed shootout that ended with a surprising twist! Let's go into the stands and ask some fans for their reactions to the contest's shocking conclusion...

DISCUSSION QUESTION 1

When Peter and Noah face off at point-blank range, they call it a draw. Would you have laid down your marker if you were one of them? Why?

DISCUSSION QUESTION 2

Do you think Mr Eccleston was right when he told his sons that you can't count on anyone but yourself? Discuss your answers.

WRITING PROMPT 1

Peter and Noah are twins. Do you know anyone who is a twin? How would your life be different if you had a twin? Would you want a twin?

WRITING PROMPT 2

Write a short story where Peter AND Noah end up joining the Royals. Are they nervous about playing on television? Do you like their new teammates? Who wins the championship? Write about it.

Sports Illustrated KIDS

INFO CENTRE

GLOSSARY

CRUEL deliberately causing pain to others

IDENTICAL exactly alike, as in identical twins

IMPATIENT in a hurry and unable to wait, or easily annoyed

MARKER main piece of equipment used in paintball. Markers use expanding gas to shoot paintballs through a barrel.

POINT-BLANK close range

SQUAD small group of people involved in the same activity, such as soldiers in the armed forces, or teammates in a sport

UNFORGIVING not willing to show mercy, or unwilling to forgive mistakes

CREATORS

SCOTT CIENCIN › Author
Scott Ciencin is a *New York Times* bestselling author of children's and adult fiction. He has written comic books, trading cards, video games and television shows, as well as many non-fiction projects. He lives in Florida, USA, with his beloved wife, Denise, and his best buddy, Bear, a golden retriever.

ABURTOV › Illustrator
Aburtov is a graphic designer and illustrator who has worked in the comic book industry for more than 11 years. In that time, Aburtov has coloured popular characters such as Wolverine, Iron Man, Punisher and Blade. He recently created his own studio called Graphikslava. Aburtov lives with his beloved wife in Monterrey, Mexico, where he enjoys spending time with family and friends.

FARES MAESE › Colourist
Fares Maese is a graphic designer and illustrator. He has worked as a colourist for Marvel Comics, and as a concept artist for the card and role-playing games Pathfinder and Warhammer. Fares loves spending time playing video games with his Graphikslava colleagues, and he's an awesome drummer.

ANDRES ESPARZA › Colourist
Andres Esparza has been a graphic designer, colourist and illustrator for many different companies and agencies. Andres now works as a full-time artist for Graphikslava studio in Monterrey, Mexico.

Sports Illustrated KIDS GRAPHIC NOVELS

QUICK COMIC

BING HAWTIN, TY TAGGART AND MATTY LYONS IN:

SKATEBOARD SONAR

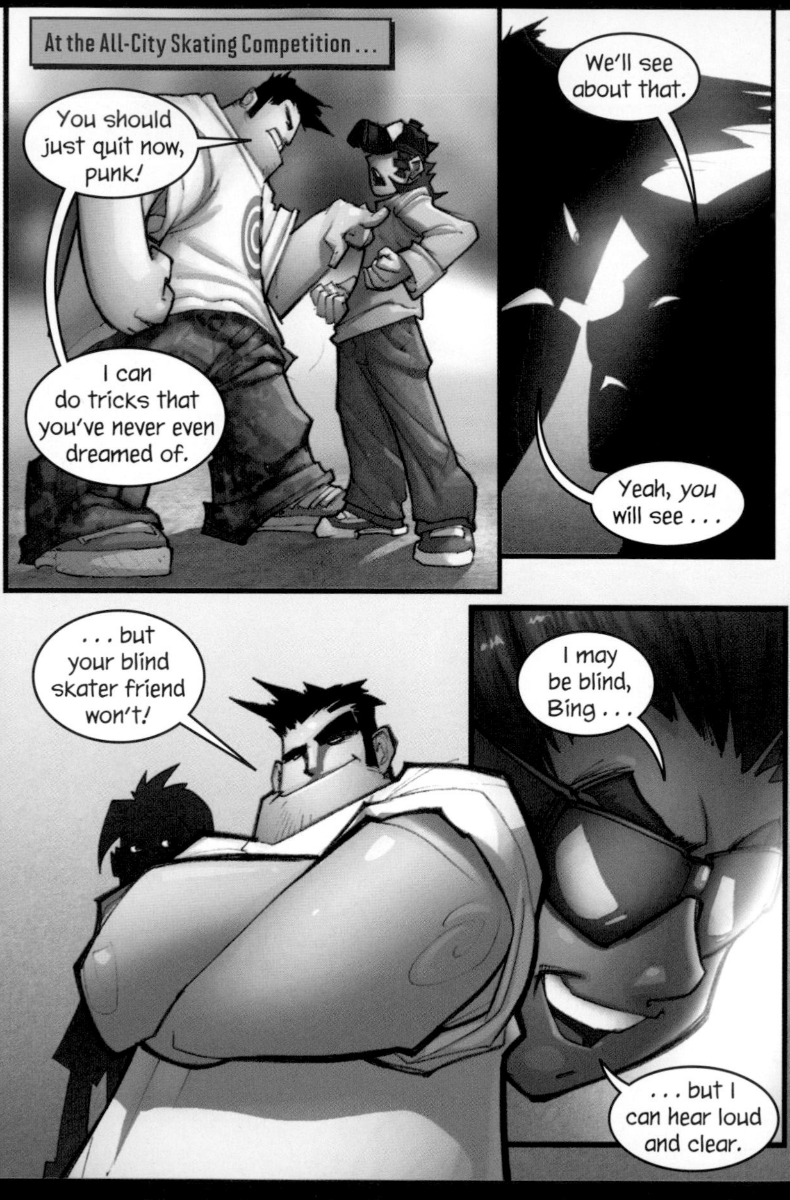
At the All-City Skating Competition . . .
You should just quit now, punk!
We'll see about that.
I can do tricks that you've never even dreamed of.
Yeah, *you* will see . . .
. . . but your blind skater friend won't!
I may be blind, Bing . . .
. . . but I can hear loud and clear.

LOVE THIS QUICK COMIC? READ THE WHOLE STORY IN *SKATEBOARD SONAR*

HOT SPORTS. HOT FORMAT!

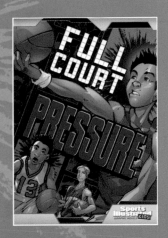

GREAT CHARACTERS BATTLE FOR SPORTS GLORY IN TODAY'S HOTTEST FORMAT—GRAPHIC NOVELS!

HOT SPORTS. HOT FORMAT!

PAINTBALL PUNK
Sports Illustrated KIDS
GRAPHIC NOVELS

Sports Illustrated KIDS
GRAPHIC NOVELS
BMX BLITZ

TRACK TEAM
TITANS
Sports Illustrated KIDS
GRAPHIC NOVELS

FULL COURT
FLASH
Sports Illustrated KIDS
GRAPHIC NOVELS

RIPTIDE
PRIDE
Sports Illustrated KIDS
GRAPHIC NOVELS

Sports Illustrated KIDS
GRAPHIC NOVELS
BMX
BREAKTHROUGH

Sports Illustrated KIDS
GRAPHIC NOVELS

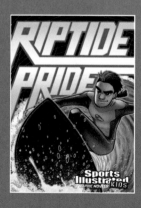

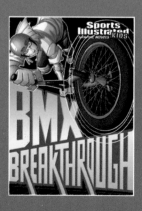